If you think I'm going to stand there while some no-brain beats my mate up . . . That lot are really in for it. Thinking they can get away with acting like that, on our patch.

Life is not easy for Stefanie. She lives in a run-down council estate which is being demolished, and her mother, a failed actress, lives in a world of her own, playing sixties pop music at full volume to mask her depression. The only thing that keeps Stefanie going is her photography—and her new relationship with Mark.

Then the brother of a schoolfriend is seriously injured in a racist attack, and Stefanie suspects Mark may be involved. Before Stefanie can reveal what she knows she has to do some serious thinking and decide exactly where her loyalties lie.

Catherine R. Johnson was born in London to Welsh/ Jamaican parents. She studied film at St Martin's School of Art and then set up a film company in East London, producing small films and videos. She wrote a screenplay for the Welsh Film Foundation, and then turned to books just before her son was born in 1991. In 1994 she won the Hackney Black Writers Competition with a short story. *In Black and White* is her first novel for Oxford University Press.

In Black and White

In Black and White

Catherine R. Johnson

OXFORD
UNIVERSITY PRESS

OXFORD
UNIVERSITY PRESS

Great Clarendon Street, Oxford OX2 6DP

Oxford University Press is a department of the University of Oxford.
It furthers the University's objective of excellence in research, scholarship,
and education by publishing worldwide in

Oxford New York

Athens Auckland Bangkok Bogotá Buenos Aires Calcutta
Cape Town Chennai Dar es Salaam Delhi Florence Hong Kong Istanbul
Karachi Kuala Lumpur Madrid Melbourne Mexico City Mumbai
Nairobi Paris São Paulo Singapore Taipei Tokyo Toronto Warsaw

and associated companies in Berlin Ibadan

Oxford is a registered trade mark of Oxford University Press
in the UK and in certain other countries

British Library Cataloguing in Publication Data available

ISBN 0 19 271829 0

Typeset by AFS Image Setters Ltd, Glasgow
Printed in Great Britain

1

Mark had kissed her last night, proper tongues in mouth stuff. It had felt interesting at the time and even more interesting when she had told Becky about it at first break. But now she wasn't so sure.

She was in the darkroom in the lower school. Stef liked the plasticky chemical smell, the funny half light from the red light bulb and the way the photos appeared like magic when you gently sloshed the fluids around in the tray. There. She picked it out carefully and put it to dry. Not bad. Close to brilliant. She liked portraits, and this was Mum and Nan foreground—on the fields by the railway arches in Spitalfields. In the background was a horse chewing grass, just off to one side. Their faces looked sad and happy at the same time, and you could tell by looking at the older woman how the lines would grow on the younger woman's face. So maybe Mum wouldn't like it that much but Nan would, and anyway Mum liked horses. Stef finished up just as Mr Bartlett, the art teacher, came in.

'Excellent work, Stefanie, really excellent!'

'It's a birthday present, for Mum and Nan. Their birthday's on the same day, see.'

'Lovely, Stefanie.'

She couldn't really tell if he meant it, but she did like Mr Bartlett a bit. As much as you could like a teacher. The Camera Club had been his idea, and it made a change to be good at something.

'Sir? Can I borrow a camera, sir, for the weekend? I want to finish the flats.'

Stefanie was working her way through her neighbours on the estate. Big black and whites. Grainy sometimes, but she thought that looked good. All the people in her block. She thought she'd arrange them in a sort of model. All the people. All together. Before the flats were demolished some time next year and they were all moved into little yellow-brick dream homes built out in the middle of nowhere.

'Ah, yes, your social document.'

'There's no writing, sir.' At least she hadn't meant there to be.

'Not that sort of document, Stefanie, I meant a record of your neighbourhood.' He smiled. 'And if you need any help, we're all here, it's wonderful to see you working so well.'

Stefanie grinned inside. She could just imagine Bartlett in the staffroom, going on to the other teachers—how he'd sorted Stefanie Clark. That was the only thing that put her off the photos sometimes: not wanting the teachers, even him, to think that any of this—*her* ideas, *her* talent— was anything to do with them. So Stefanie just nodded. She needed the school camera and the stupid blobby light meter and the school darkroom. Keep them sweet.

'No problem, Stefanie, of course.'

Stefanie tucked the camera into the bottom of her

schoolbag and ducked out under the blackout curtain and out through the door. She didn't want to stop and talk now, even though Bartlett was all right. She'd spent half the lunch hour already in the dark, and Becky would be waiting.

But by the time she made it over to the upper building, lunch was over. Becky was standing by the doorway to the girls loos, scratching into the brick with her library badge. It said 'Keeley Matthews kisses roaches'.

Stef groaned, 'That's awful, Beck.'

'Good though, innit. I was going to put snogs, but then I thought that Keeley went with kisses. Sort of rhymes.'

'Really poetic, Beck.'

'Yeah, that's it! Keeley kisses, Stefanie snogs . . . '

'And Becky . . . '

'Becky gets a bollocking for being late . . . '

'It's only PDS.'

Personal Development Studies. Stef had read it on the timetable, but what it really meant was how to fill in forms, how to avoid sexually transmitted diseases, hanging around arcades, drugs, and any other antisocial behaviour. It usually took the form of a discussion that degenerated into some form of chaos: shouting, giggling, throwing things. Stefanie usually spent the time doodling little spirals or thorny sided squares, and talking, quietly at least, to Becky.

'Stefanie Clark, Rebecca Oliver, I like my classes to start on time.'

'Sorry, Miss Sanders.'

'Racism in London' said the blackboard. Becky rolled her eyes.

'It's racism again.'

'If you have something to say, Becky, why not say it to the whole class?'

Becky sat down, taking her time.

'Can't we do family planning, Miss? We're always doing racism.'

Shahnaz, in the front row, turned on her. 'It's important, Miss, tell her.'

Becky mimed a yawn, some of the white girls laughed. Stefanie turned off—just like she'd learned to in English and Maths. Outside she could see the traffic on the main road into the city and, because it was Friday, crowds of men on the street coming out of the mosque.

'And this area of London has always had a migrant population . . .'

Miss Sanders's words drifted in and out of focus. She'd heard it all before, Huguenots from France, Jews from Eastern Europe, and now Pakistanis and Bengalis. It looked a mess outside: dirty, fuggy with traffic and rubbish. Stef couldn't understand why anyone would want to make it halfway across the world for *this* . . . Stef stared. Two girls—they could be women—veiled head to toe, were waiting at the bus stop. Blowing shocking pink bubbles of bubblegum. Bright like flowers against the black of their dress.

A bus passed, wiping the picture like an edit on a film. Stef turned back to the class. Shahnaz was talking, almost shouting, about fighting back, about not being passive. Some of the girls at the back were reading *J-17* under the desk. Stefanie drew 'M. B.' for Mark Brody on the back of her neat English book then scribbled it out in case anyone noticed.

At the desk nearest the door Amina Begum fiddled with her hair: a thick black ponytail tied with a glittery purple elastic. Stef watched. She was splitting the ends, only stopping when the electric bell sounded for the end of class. Amina lived in Stef's flats but they never walked home together. Stef kidded herself that it was because Amina was such a boffin. But she knew that wasn't the truth. Stefanie hadn't photographed Amina's family either. She hadn't yet knocked on their door, or on that of the people downstairs with the green Arabic sticker above the door. She only had those families and nutty Mrs Menzies who fed the cats left to do. This weekend, she thought to herself, watching Amina's heavy, shiny hair swing round behind her.

'Coming round, Stef?' Becky grinned. 'Or are you busy?'

'Don't be soft, Beck.'

'Not seeing Mark, then?'

Stefanie blushed. She'd been thinking Mark might knock for her, but then it would be better to be out being mysterious, not just waiting in for him.

'I'll be round later, all right?'

Stef could feel the school camera in her bag, banging against her leg as she ran down the school stairs. One of the things she didn't like about the school cameras was the huge glob of yellow paint and the 'Property of Stepney Square School' sticker. She would have liked her own. Something matt-black and interesting. The last two Christmases she had hinted, given up hinting and then asked, blatantly, obviously, begged even, but no luck. She'd even seen one that would do in Mum's catalogue; you know, £2.50 every week for the rest of your life. No camera though.

Mum said, 'That nice Mr Bartlett said you can always use the school's, and if I bought you one it would only get sat on or nicked, or you'd be over cameras and it would be in the bottom of the wardrobe with the ice skates.'

Stef shivered. The ice skates always made her feel guilty. Just the sight of the plastic bag they were in made her insides turn over. Once, it seemed years ago now, she and Leona had gone up the leisure centre every week skating. It was miles on the bus but they had really been into it. Stefanie wasn't bad, she could skate backwards and forwards and do some smart turns. And it was a laugh.

Then Mum and Nan had got her the boots, white boots, like in those corny girls' books and comics, and it was like every dream coming true all at once. Stefanie even slept with the boots by the side of the bed, so they were the first things she'd see when she opened her eyes. And Stefanie had wanted those boots badly, like an ache. A really deep ache. But they never went skating now. Mum just didn't understand. The skating thing was over. It wasn't like photography. Stefanie knew that, but she couldn't explain. Mum said they should sell the boots but just talking about them made her feel shaky.

So she was stuck with a Stepney Square Girls' School Special, a relic from the seventies, all scratched chrome and battered plastic, with a click as loud as a car backfiring in the next street. The camera thumped into her thigh extra hard and Stef could picture the blue-yellow bruise opening like a flower on her leg.

Her estate wasn't far, it should have only taken Stefanie ten minutes door to door. But as she crossed the Commercial Road she could see the knots of Shadwell boys coming north, walking wide and easy so they took up most of the pavement. There were two groups, fifteen boys in all, Stef counted. They were talking too loud and shouting at people. As soon as she saw them Stefanie ducked into the post office hoping they'd pass. There was a kid, Year Seven by the look of her, from the Ursuline Convent hovering by the Jiffy bags. An easy target in brown and yellow. Stefanie felt sorry for her, at least Stepney Girls' uniform wasn't that obvious. Both girls watched as the boys passed the post office and headed towards Bethnal Green.

'They're going to fight the Bishop Arnold boys,' the convent girl whispered. 'It's been really bad since Easter.'

Stef nodded. She knew all this already. Where did this kid think she'd been? Venus?

'Are you walking towards Watney Market?' The Year Seven girl looked hopeful.

'Almost . . . ' Stefanie felt sorry for her. 'Come on, we can go together.'

Stefanie's estate had been scheduled for demolition. They'd pulled one of the low rise blocks down before Christmas and now they were taking the big tower block apart, piece by piece. Too many people living nearby to blow it up. Stefanie could see less of the building every day as the outside panels were lifted away by a giant crane, revealing a metal skeleton building. Sad and anorexic.

Stefanie's block was a low rise. Three storeys with three flats on each landing; not pretty, but Stefanie knew she'd miss it. Mum wanted the move, wanted to be out of Stepney, to be somewhere else. Anywhere else. But to Stefanie these were her flats, and they felt like home.

She could hear the music as soon as she turned into the car park behind the flats. Mrs Menzies, who lived on the ground floor, banged on the window at her.

'Tell that mother of yours to shut it or I'm fetching the environmental health on her.'

Stef smiled a nice girly smile, and kicked the assortment of cat feeding bowls that littered the area round Mrs Menzies's door.

'Oops, sorry.'

Mrs Menzies glared and Stef ran up the steps to her landing. Mum was playing 'Come Go With Me' by the Staples Singers, an ancient soul tune. It meant that Mum wouldn't be totally hysterical, like if it was Aretha or Dionne Warwick. But still, Stef couldn't be entirely sure of her mother's mood. By the time she'd reached the door the music was deafening. Stef fished the key out from under her school shirt and went in.

'Mum! Mum, give it a rest.' Even shouting she wasn't sure Mum could hear her.

Mum was standing in the front room swaying slightly, her hands over her face, but Stef knew she was weeping. The Whitmore twins, Danny and Dean, were sitting on the brown leatherette sofa in front of the telly. Dean was crying too. Stef picked Dean up and sat him on her hip, turned the stereo down, and hugged her mother. She felt her mother's wet cold cheek against her own.

'Mum?' She rubbed her back. 'What is it with you, hey?'

Mum's famous shiny strawberry-blonde hair was tied back and twisted into some kind of knot, secured with a pencil. Her trademark green eyes were red rimmed, and the brown velvet eyeliner smudged. Stef had none of her mother's looks, she was Daddy's girl. Her skin was too freckly, her darker brown hair too curly. Her eyes weren't as green as Mum's either. Stef liked to kid herself sometimes, but she was no Carole Clark.

The only jobs Mum got through the agency these days were as canteen lady in *The Bill*, or walk-ons in gritty London dramas. She was the woman who walked by as the building burst into flames, the cheery stallholder, that kind of thing. That's why she looked after the Whitmore twins.

'Marry rich, love,' said her mother still swaying.

Stef thought to herself that she wasn't marrying at all as she put Dean back next to his brother in front of some cartoon about mice on motorbikes from outer space. The door of her room was open.

'Mum! You let them in! I told you not to let them in!'

Three boxes of photos had been pulled open and shaken like confetti all over the floor. She would have liked to throw the Whitmore twins over the balcony, making sure they landed head first in Mrs Menzies's fly encrusted cat food bowls. And her mother after them. Stefanie allowed herself five minutes' dreamtime 'when I live on my own', then she started scooping up the photos, looking at them as she put them away. There were some from when she'd started camera club, more than two years ago. Her and Becky and Leona mucking around. Posing in the park like models. But apart from Leona, who really did have long legs, they just looked like a bunch of fat twelve year olds in horrible clothes. Sad, thought Stefanie.

And there were some truly sad landscapes Mr Bartlett had made them do: 'The Changing Environment'. Total crap idea, Stefanie remembered. Then she found the photos she had taken later of the cars streaming out of the Rotherhithe tunnel at night. Hell's mouth, Nan called it.

There were the ones she'd taken over the Easter holidays. Portraits—big heads staring out at you from their white frames. They were the start of it—the start of her big idea of getting everyone in the flats, all photoed and pinned down. Even Mrs Menzies, even an old bag like her. Everyone. Even the picture of the Whitmore twins looked good she thought—but that was probably the superhero masks. Stef felt better. She was good. Everyone knew that now.

Mum in her work face, Carole Clark, aspiring actress/model. Only she'd been aspiring for so long, as long as Stefanie could remember. Even when she'd been the lollipop lady and worked afternoons in the Turkish newsagents, she had still told everyone she was just waiting for a call from her agent. Mum liked to be carefully lit, she said. But the best picture of Mum was a surprise. Stefanie had been standing at the end of the landing waiting to see if Leona was coming out when Mum came out with the twins. She had picked up Danny and kissed him. Gotcha, thought Stef. And she had. Mum looked sad and lost, and one hundred times more beautiful than on her agency cards, or when she'd been the Lord Mayor's daughter in *Dick Whittington* at the Edmonton Apollo in 1976.

But Mum always looked more real and more pretty in photos than she did in real life. 'Pretend, I can do,' was her favourite sentence. 'Don't ask me to do real life,' she'd say, 'pretend I can do.' Stefanie thought her mother severely lacking when it came to real life.

Stefanie didn't want her photos to be like that—to be pretend. All happy colours and smiling faces. Bright lights and camera tricks. She wanted real life. Black and white.

Stef put the photos away. 'How do I look, darling?' Mum's other favourite sentence. Stef mouthed it at herself in the mirror. She couldn't look that bad or Mark Brody would never have kissed her. She started to smile, then a truly horrible idea swept over her. Unless it was for a dare. The thought was so awful Stef almost retched.

Stefanie put on her jeans and went out. Mum had started on 'Twenty Motown Greats' and Stefanie knew that she was a lost cause. 'I'm going to Beck's,' she shouted from the front door. Last night in her diary she had written, 'Mum is mad.' She'd read it again this morning and it seemed the only thing that was real about her.

2

It was a fairly long walk over to Becky's but Stefanie liked it. She liked getting out of the flat and off the dying estate. Sometimes, like today, she ran nearly all the way, dodging through the end of the market which always smelled of coriander, past another mosque, and up across the main road.

Becky lived on the Crown Estate, posh because it wasn't council. Tiny squares of gardens in between the flats and little brown brick maisonettes with ruffly pink curtains in the windows. There was a man who swept the path and removed most of the dog-do and locked the metal gates after dark.

The estate was built right up against the park and sometimes the park seemed to spill over into the estate. There were squirrels and birds you never saw in the streets. Stefanie recognized the magpies, but there were other, stranger birds as well. *Exotics*, Becky's mum called them— lost on their migration somewhere else. Stefanie couldn't understand why they would want to stop *here*, of all places: in the middle of a dirty smelly city. But Becky's mother explained it was all the food—and the warmth from the buildings.

'Becky do you think my mum is crazy?'

Stefanie lay half on Becky's bed reading a magazine on the floor and eating her way through a packet of chocolate gypsy creams. Becky's mum always had biscuits—even a proper biscuit tin: co-ordinated and flowery to match the kettle. Stefanie never had biscuits at home. Her mum was always 'Watching my figure, love, or no one else will.'

Becky's bedroom was bluebell white. She had painted it herself in the holidays and there were plenty of lumpy dried drips where she had been over generous with the paint.

'No. You know.' Stefanie sat up. 'Really mad—nuts, like.'

Becky was curling her eyelashes; this involved clamping them in a kind of hand-held waffle iron. Stef didn't like the look of it, but Becky assured her it really worked.

Becky smiled. 'Not totally fruit loopy, no.'

Becky's family were so normal it hurt. Her brother, Martin, was still at school. Her mother was a school secretary and her dad worked in the parks for the council. Driving round chaining the swings up at night.

Becky finished the other eye. 'How do I look?' She batted her new curly lashes furiously. 'Snog magnet or what?'

Stefanie giggled.

''S all right for you,' Becky said, rubbing a spot on her chin with a dob of concealer.

'What d'you mean?'

'Come off it! Mark, Mark Brody, remember him?'

'Your chin's all honey beige and the rest of your face is Becky Oliver,' Stefanie said, spraying the carpet with chocolate crumbs.

Becky faced the mirror. 'Look, I'm blending it in, aren't I? And don't change the subject.'

Stefanie didn't want to not talk about Mark. But now, nearly a day later, she felt there was nothing much left to say. He'd met her up by the triangle, on her way home from the Chinese, fetching Mum's favourite Singapore noodles. Then he walked back with her, even though it was totally in the wrong direction for Mark's.

They hadn't said much. He had his hands in his pockets and his shoulders were hunched up, and Stefanie couldn't quite bear to look directly at his face. Into his eyes. She couldn't think what to say. Concentrated instead on making sure the steam from the hot food didn't burn her arms and on the way the cracks in the pavement joined and parted like railway lines.

Mark was seventeen. Stefanie liked the idea of being seventeen. You could be out of school. She imagined herself taller by then, two extra years of growth, and more sussed, more cool. She imagined herself as a photographic prodigy, sitting in the office of some big magazine, being offered as much money as she wanted just to take pictures all day every day. And maybe even turning jobs down.

Mark was at college, she knew that. He hung out with Lee and Gavin. The Gavin that Becky used to go with. She'd gone up the college with Beck, waiting for him. It was a bit scary, everyone being older—not just the security guards—and they'd had to sit outside the canteen trying not to look like schoolgirls.

Stefanie knew Mark was good looking. Everyone said so, so it must be true. And he was interested in her. She still couldn't quite believe it. He said she was nice, in the way that boys do, and when he'd kissed her, backed up against the sari shop round the corner, Stefanie hadn't wanted him to stop. He didn't taste of beer or prawn Skips, which was what Becky said Gavin always tasted of. And the skin on his neck, which she felt with her free hand, was hot and soft. She'd almost dropped the Singapore noodles. As it was, the bag with the prawn crackers slithered to the ground and she had to pull away from him. Then it was just embarrassing. Stefanie had mumbled something about being in a hurry and had run the rest of the way home, flushed and grinning.

'So what are you smiling at?' Becky had finished her face and was screwing her feet into a pair of trainers.

Becky's mum was sitting in front of the downstairs window, head down, zigzagging a knitting machine to and fro.

'What are you making, Mrs Oliver?' Stefanie liked being polite to other people's mothers. She could tell Becky's mum didn't really like her—blamed her for Becky's bad marks and attitude. If you only knew, Stef thought, staring at her. She was using flecky blue and white wool, a kind of dirty baby boy colour, and the fabric seemed to be oozing out of the far side of the machine like a tidal wave of fluff. But Stef felt the knitting anyway and smiled as if she liked it.

Mrs Oliver looked up. 'Like it?' Stefanie nodded back at her.

'It's for Rebecca's big cousin, Janice. You know, for her birthday.'

'Lovely,' said Stefanie trying to sound convincing, 'No, it's really nice.'

Becky stood in the doorway and mimed being sick.

Stefanie had to wait for Becky by the front door. Becky had changed her top three times already but she still checked herself one last time in the hall mirror. Pulling the

T-shirt out of the waist of her jeans, and then tucking it back in again.

'Come on, Beck, it'll be dark if you don't move it!'

'I'm coming, all right.' Becky smoothed her hair back from her face. 'See you, Mum.'

The park was big and flat. Not so long ago, but before Stefanie could remember, there'd been houses here. Little terraced houses that people liked living in, at least that's what Mum said. Then they'd all been knocked down to make this dead flat, unhappy looking patch of green.

There was a good kids' playground though and even if they were too old for it now, it was where they met up sometimes, after school. To muck around on the swings gabbing and that.

On the far side of the park the canal ran straight, like a road, on its way to the river, and beyond that Canary Wharf like a bad mistake about to fall over. There was a group of kids playing football on the hard scuffed-up grass and although it was only May it was warm as a decent July.

Stefanie's arms were already going brown and the little hairs were golden from hanging around outside the flats, or in the park, or outside the Chinese chippie by the traffic lights.

'What's that?' Stefanie pointed at the skeleton of a stage in the middle of the park.

'It's a stage, innit.'

'I can see that.'

'There's some do or something, tomorrow, Saturday.'

'Any good?'

'Dunno.' Becky shrugged and pulled out her bubblegum as far as it would go and both girls changed direction slightly, drifting towards the stage. It had a small fence of crash barriers around it and banners hung from it which read 'Stepney Multi-Cultural Festival' and Saturday's date.

'It's a Paki thing.' Becky blew a big pink bubble.

'Becky!' Stefanie looked around. 'It's not like that!'

Becky grinned. 'Innit? You bet they'll have some crap Paki singers or something and that's it. Oh, and maybe a crap reggae band, but nothing no one likes, nothing no one wants.'

Stefanie wanted to say something. 'They're not all from Pakistan, you know,' was about the best she could manage. She wished Becky wasn't like that sometimes, was more . . . she sighed. Becky was her friend, and that was what mattered.

'Upset you, have I? Dear, dear, you've been hanging out with Bartlett, in the Art room, "celebrating our multi-cultural borough". It's all crap. No one wants to be multi-cultural, do they, really? Really all mixed in. I mean, like school, it's the Pakis—'

'They're not "Pakis".'

'You know what I mean, the Pakis and the rest.'

'So you wouldn't mind being a nigger, then?'

'I'm not black enough, am I?' Becky grinned.

'Not white enough either, and your dad's black, what does that make you? Apart from stroppy.'

'Yeah, half-caste power.' Becky laughed. 'Say it loud, I'm beige and I'm proud.'

'You just make a joke of it, don't you?'

'So what do you know, anyway, white girl? You swallow all this multi-culture shit, and think it's all right. Just 'cause people don't say Paki out loud doesn't mean they don't think it. How can it be better if people still think like it? How many "Asian" girls do you hang with? It's all racist, everywhere, everything.' Becky shook her head and kissed her teeth, the way her dad did.

16

'OK, I know nothing. I just wish people would be nice to each other, you know.'

'Oh, yeah, right, Stefanie Clark says, end racism, be nice.' Becky smiled. 'I wish I was on your planet, Stef, I really do. Planet nice. I think that's worse, just pretending to be nice. Just pretending.'

Stefanie opened her mouth but said nothing. Becky was right, she was pretending, just like Mum.

'Forget it, Stef, let's just forget it.'

Becky slipped through the crash barriers and up on to the platform.

'What are you doing, Beck? Get down!'

Becky was doing the routine she'd seen some girl group doing on MTV. It involved a lot of shaking, and excited pouting, and Stefanie was red with laughter.

'You're killing me, Beck!'

'Come on, come on, I'm the lead singer with all that hair and blue contact lenses.' Becky spun round. 'No, no wait up! I'll be the other one! You know! She goes out with that footballer. And you're taking my picture—go on, Stef. Go on!'

Stefanie wiped her eyes.

'Go on, Stef!'

Stefanie lifted up the school camera. 'I'm only wasting three shots on you, you know.'

Becky had some front. Stefanie admired that, she would never have the nerve to stand up there, with people walking past looking at you and that. That was one of the best things about the camera. It meant she could join in things just by watching. She could be a part of whatever was going on without actually risking herself. Stefanie found the camera perfect to hide behind. So she did.

'There.' Stefanie wound on the film. 'That's it, you can stop now.'

'But, darling,' Becky blew Stefanie an overblown kiss,

17

'I was only just getting started.' Becky did a few more moves, spun round and sat down, dangling her legs off the stage. Stefanie joined her, she felt less nervous. If someone was going to come along and chuck them off the stage, it would have happened by now. It was nice being high up, looking out over the park and across to the gas holders on the other side of the canal. Stefanie liked London. She would have liked a big house, like the ones she'd seen on a school trip to Kew Gardens, but that was still London.

Across the park, the football match was breaking up. A gang of boys drifted over from the main road towards the playground and jumped the fence. In the middle of the park was a paved circle with benches, sheltered by beds of spindly bushes. The bins there were all melted and collapsed where people had started fires in them. The sky looked sort of yellow—pollution, Becky said. And high up you could make out the vapour trails of jumbo jets, leaving for Greece or Australia, Stefanie thought. She'd never been to those places, but she knew she'd go one day. She couldn't hear the noise of the aeroplanes above the traffic. Friday was always bad, and the main road heading for Essex was solid.

It was so warm. Stefanie walked over to the ice cream van parked up by the gate and bought one of those mango lollies with ice cream in the middle. She was almost back at the stage when it happened. Stef could see Becky swinging her legs and blowing bubbles when a boy, bare chested, sped past her pushing into her.

'Watch yourself!' Stefanie shouted at him but he'd ducked into the spiky bushes. The school camera was sent flying up into the air and Stefanie had to sacrifice her lolly to save it. She caught the camera but the lolly splatted on the grey path. Stefanie kicked it over with the toe of her trainer. It was encrusted with lumpy gravel and sweet wrappers like a caddis fly larva case.

Stefanie glared after the boy, but he had gone. She could still smell him though, smell his sweat hanging in the air where he had just been. Suddenly Becky was waving at her from the stage. Stef couldn't make out what Becky was saying so she shook her head at her. Becky pointed towards the playground. Stef shrugged, she couldn't see anything. Then, three more boys came up the path in school shirts and black trousers: Shadwell boys. Bishop Arnold were grey and Saddlers were navy so they had to be Shadwell boys. Shadwell boys hate Stepney girls, thought Stefanie, and the way the taller boy's white school shirt was half pulled out of his trousers made her scared. She edged to the side of the path and tried to hide the camera in her hands.

They looked like dogs. The sort of dogs you pretend not to be scared of so they don't bite you. Black hair, black trousers, brown skin, black and tan, black and tan like Dobermans. Doberboys.

Shadwell boys hate Stepney girls. No, maybe it was *do* Stepney girls. Stefanie felt a little moustache of sweat coming on her top lip. One of their trainers squished on the lolly sending an ooze of white stuff out over the path.

That was when Stefanie realized they weren't looking at her at all. A noise in the bushes sent them plunging into the shrubbery. Wading through, shouting at each other, barking, until they flushed the bare-chested boy out into the open. He was criss-crossed with scratches bursting into shiny bubbles of dark red blood on his pink white skin. His eyes looked blank. Stefanie wished herself invisible.

He ran on again, half slipping on the gravel and over towards the canal. Stefanie stopped watching when the two other boys caught up with him, shut her eyes and ears and ran back to Becky, watching from the stage.

'What's that about, then?' Becky was on tiptoe straining

to see, but they had dragged the half naked boy out of sight. The girls could still hear him, though.

'Do you want to go and look?'

'Are you joking, Beck?' Stefanie was already feeling guilty. 'Call an ambulance more like.'

'He was from Bishop Arnold. Like Martin.'

'The bare one?'

'The white one.'

Suddenly Stefanie felt too cold in her T-shirt. A wind seemed to be blowing up from somewhere. Maybe from the river at the end of the canal. Maybe near the bottom of the river it was cold and dark, and the cold was rising up and towards them. She could see Becky had goose pimples too.

It was a long time before the noise stopped.

'I wish they wouldn't. I mean, haven't those boys got anything better to do?'

Becky jumped down off the stage. 'No,' she said.

It was quiet walking back to Becky's. Even the topic of whether Mark was going to see her again, and if she should phone him first, or wait for him to phone her, didn't fill the quiet up enough.

'Do you think Martin knew him, that boy?' Stef asked.

Becky shrugged. 'Dunno, he might've done. They're always at it, that lot. Martin says they go up Shadwell of a lunch time and wait for them.' She spat out her bubblegum, thoughtfully. 'Shadwell boys are the worst, though.'

Stefanie agreed. 'I saw some after school today. Walking round like they own the place, scaring little kids.'

'See you tomorrow, then, Stef.' Becky didn't look round. 'Unless you're out with Mark.'

'Oh yeah.'

By the time Stefanie got home Mum was sitting on the

sofa clutching a cushion to her middle. She was blowing cigarette smoke up into the air, which curled in and out of the metal light fitting. On the telly *Brookside* was just ending. At least the Motown had stopped, Stefanie thought.

Mum didn't look up. Stefanie hovered near the telly. Mum still said nothing, and normally Stef would have taken the hint and retreated to her bedroom.

'Anyone call for me, Mum?'

Mum said nothing.

'No one knock for me?' She tried again.

'No, love, no one.'

Stef thought she might as well just go to bed. She had a book Mr Bartlett had got for her from the library. It was photographs—a French photographer with two names that Stefanie had never heard of, but the photos were really good. Really good, just like real life. Sad and happy, but mostly sad. Some of them made her cry. An empty street or something. Nothing she could pin down. But the tears came, and she had to shut the book so that the tears fell on the wipe-clean plastic cover. Stefanie wanted *her* pictures to make people cry.

She lay in bed, even though it was not quite dark, imagining her model estate. Her photos—her work—all put together and on display in a precious glass box. Maybe in the school foyer. She checked herself. No—not the school—that art gallery up by the big roundabout before you get into the city. That's where it should go. She had been on a school trip there more than once. Stefanie thought it was because the girls could walk and that meant it was cheap. The art was useless most of the time: jaggedy metal sculptures that looked like the stuff people stick in the top of walls to stop anyone climbing over, or paintings of hard little shapes—not even people—and hard colours. Stefanie knew she could do better than that.

3

It was a perfect morning. Even the half demolished tower block looked good. All you could see was the naked lift shaft—a finger poking through a mesh of metal skeleton. Stefanie could just see it through a crack in the curtains. She rolled over and made a frame for it with her fingers and took a pretend photo. Only two more sets of photos to do and she'd be finished. Well, half finished. In a way the pictures were just the beginning and a part of her felt quite scared it wouldn't all work out. The idea was so perfect—so formed in her head that maybe it wouldn't work in real life. Stefanie got up. She was being stupid now. Take the pictures and get on with it. Not like Mum—always waiting for things to happen to her.

Mum wasn't up, so Stef did the washing up from yesterday, found a cereal box that still had some cereal in and made breakfast. Stef took Mum her tea the way she used to and sat on the edge of her bed, stroking her forehead and watching the breaths make her body rise and fall under the duvet. She wondered what Mum dreamed about. Acting maybe, or a big house with cleaners and walk-in wardrobes. A feature in *Hello* and a part in *EastEnders*. A pretend life with a good soundtrack. Stef kissed her, softly so that she wouldn't wake and went out.

Amina first, Stefanie thought, then pressed the doorbell a couple of times. She stepped back leaning against the landing wall and looking down into the car park. Mrs Menzies was standing on her front step calling to her cat family. Stefanie watched as she scraped out a tin of pinkish cat meat for them.

No one answered the door but Stef knew someone had to be in because the kitchen window was open a crack and she could hear the telly going, or a tape maybe. She rang again. She couldn't hear a bell noise, so she knocked hard.

But it wasn't Amina. It was a boy—her big brother—skinny and twice as tall as Amina with the vague wispy shadow of a moustache on his top lip. She couldn't remember his name, and looked past him for Amina. Even though close up he looked fairly weedy, she knew he was in with one of the big gangs and that Mum was always polite to him. He was always with at least two or three other boys just hanging around. They were older boys from other estates. They wore black nylon jackets, but then to be honest so did everyone else. They hung around talking. Laughing after you'd just walked past. Looking right at you and leering.

Leona said, once, some boy—was it Amina's brother?—some boy had grabbed her tit as she went past. Leona had swung her school bag at him and it was good because it'd been a Thursday which meant Biology, so she had a good lot of heavy books in it. Right across the face she got him. But then a week or so later some boys had stopped her in the park and thrown her bag in the canal. She went home the long way now and walked with Maria and Esther who were both really hard.

Stefanie knew Amina's brother had left Shadwell a year or two ago. Funny how the Asian boys all went there even though Bishop Arnold was nearer. She also heard from someone that he had two gold teeth and how had he paid for them when he'd only just started signing on? And they had Sky.

Stefanie didn't know about the gold teeth but she had seen the satellite dish. But nearly everyone had satellite or cable now anyway so that didn't mean much.

'She's not in.' He wore metal framed boffin glasses like Amina and the sunlight bounced right off them. Stefanie couldn't see his eyes, only the reflection of the skeleton tower block beyond the flats. Stefanie thought that'd look good in a photo.

'I'm in Amina's class at school.' Stefanie's script had gone seriously wrong. She had expected Amina—or at least her dad who she could have smiled at and been polite to. She couldn't think what to say. No one said anything. Stefanie fiddled with the camera in her hands and tried harder to remember his name.

'She's not in.' He said it again, slower.

'I wanted to take some photos.' She held up her camera. 'It's a project, for school.' More silence. 'Shall I come back?'

The boy's face cracked into a grin, 'You're Stefanie, you're the one who takes pictures.' Stefanie tried to look for any gold teeth but had to stop herself being too obvious. He might think she was totally mad.

Stefanie smiled, the camera always made things easier. She relaxed. 'I'll take yours, if you like.' She thought the light hitting the wall and the dark of the flat inside would look good. The reflective boffin glasses looked good too. 'I'll take it now.'

'All right.' The boy took off his glasses and his eyes were all screwed up in the sunlight.

'No, keep them on, they look really good.'

He propped himself up in the doorway, filling the door frame. He had a white T-shirt on and his skin and hair were dark, his skin darker than his sister's. Stefanie took a few shots and said she'd come back.

'I want a picture of you all, you know, all together, if that's OK.'

'Yeah, OK, sure. I'll sort it with Dad.' And he shut the door.

'The one who takes pictures.' She liked that, maybe he was all right really. Or at least as all right as he could be.

Mrs Menzies straightened up in the courtyard and called, 'Puss puss puss pu-uss'. Stefanie leant over the landing wall—it would be a good shot; Menzies bent over double in a sea of cats. Then she remembered that Mr Bartlett had said she should always ask first. But she took a couple of pictures anyway and then went down the stairs. They were old tiled stairs that didn't smell too bad and weren't too mucky. She stood at the bottom of the stairwell watching and working herself up to be polite.

'Mrs Menzies?' she said it in her sweetest, 'I'm such a nice girl' voice. 'Mrs Menzies? It's me, Stefanie, from upstairs.'

Mrs Menzies straightened up. The smell that wafted out of the open door of her flat was of old lady and cat. Stefanie didn't get too close. 'I'd like to take some pictures, for school.' Mrs Menzies looked unconvinced. 'Of you, and the cats if you like.' Stefanie thought to herself that it would be completely bogus to take a picture of Mrs Menzies without the cats. She grinned like a happy child at the old woman. She considered offering to do the old bat's shopping, or maybe even go up the post office. Surely Mrs Menzies couldn't refuse, could she?

The corners of Mrs Menzies's mouth disappeared into heavy folds of skin at each side, as if she had never ever in her life smiled. Now it looked as if it would be impossible for the muscles in her face to move any way at all. They were set completely. Stefanie had seen her mother sitting in front of her dressing table. Mum had one with lights all round the edge—she said it was professional—moving her face around, arching her eyebrows, widening her eyes, pursing and opening her mouth, then rubbing under her chin and examining her neck. 'It's always a woman's neck that goes first, love.'

Stefanie couldn't see if Mrs Menzies had a neck, but she was sure it would have gone. Stefanie thought that maybe in some ways, ways to do with which brand of conditioner made your hair really shiny, or how to do eyeliner straight off in one blob-free line, then Mum wasn't entirely crazy. Maybe Stefanie should start smiling more in case one day she couldn't.

Mrs Menzies said nothing.

'I'm doing everyone, taking their pictures, you know, before we move out. I could show you some that I've done if you like.'

Mrs Menzies bent down again and continued scraping out cat food into more saucers.

'It won't take a minute.' Stefanie was beginning to get desperate. 'Please? I'll make sure you get a copy.' What more could the old bat possibly want? A gold frame, a before and after make-over session like in those magazines? 'And here we have Mrs Menzies after the complete head transplant . . . '

'Just the one picture, Mrs Menzies, please?'

Stefanie lifted the camera up.

Mrs Menzies picked up the empty tins and slammed the door of her flat.

'I take it that's a no, then,' Stefanie called from outside.

'You bet that's a no,' the old lady shouted back. 'I know what you think of me. And I'm not having you taking the piss and have the world and his wife laugh at me. No thank you.'

Stefanie flushed. The old woman was right, maybe she could read minds, maybe that's why old women could be witches. They'd have burned her, Stef thought. She went hot and shaky and made a promise to herself never to kick the old bat's cat bowls. Then she realized Hosna and her little sisters were leaning over the balcony on the second floor giggling, so she took their picture instead and ran upstairs and back into the flat.

Mum was in the kitchen lighting up her first fag of the day. She didn't have her make-up on and she was leaning by the window watching Hosna and her sisters trail off to the shops.

'Look at her,' Mum pointed with her cigarette. 'That poor kid's old already.'

Hosna was pushing the little one—Rumi—in a buggy. The older two shuffled along, one on each side.

'It's work experience.' Stef clicked the kettle on.

'You've got to have fun, love. Have a life.'

'And you'd know about that.'

'I had a life.'

'Yeah and I ruined it. Is that what you're saying?'

'No, love. No, love. Not like that.' Mum kissed her teeth and pushed the hair up out of her face. She was looking older these days.

'Like what, then?'

'Things change, people change.' What a stupid empty rubbish thing for Mum to say, Stefanie thought.

She looked out of the window. As far as she could see it was only *things* that changed. Buildings went up and down. Shops opened and shut but Mum only ever got worse and Stefanie was always the one who cleaned up after her.

'So why don't you change, then?'

Mum said nothing. Just stared out of the window following Hosna until she turned the corner out of sight. Mum was so hopeless. Stefanie often thought that it would be a good idea to get people to pass a test before they let you have children. Mum would have failed.

Stefanie went back into her room and shut the door then took down the box of pictures of her neighbours. She had shots of everyone outside their front doors, and then another picture inside. In the kitchen or the front room— smiling sometimes—little kids making faces to be stupid. Jabida and Sohail downstairs mucking around. The nurses who lived next door to Mrs Menzies in their uniforms. Mrs Kaur with the buggy that seemed surgically attached— there was always some other new baby in it. Even one of herself and Mum. She'd done it on the timer, setting the camera up balanced on the landing ledge, then she'd run round to stand next to Mum and look daughterly. Stef was taller than her mother now and her nose was practically the same, but she never looked pretty as her mother did. Never photographed like Mum. She laid the photos all out on the rug by her bed. There were still two gaps, Amina's and Menzies. Amina would be cool, but she couldn't think what to do about Mrs Menzies. Maybe it was just a bad day. Maybe Menzies would come round later on. Maybe if she had seen the other pictures she wouldn't mind.

The whole thing, the whole layout, would look daft with a hole where Mrs Menzies should be. Maybe she'd die and they'd get someone else in. What a mean idea, Stefanie told herself. What a mean un-nice idea. She liked to think of herself as kind and helpful. Put upon by her selfish immature mother. That's how she pictured it. But what if that wasn't true? What if she'd end up bitter and dippy just like Carole Clark. Maybe she was headed that way already.

Stef watched Amina and her dad coming through the car park that afternoon. Amina had her big hoody coat on even though it was warm and her hair swung behind her as she walked. She didn't look anything like her brother. She looked like her dad though—he was small too—and he smiled at her as they walked along. Stefanie would've liked a dad like that. But then, she couldn't imagine anyone choosing to live with her mother. Least of all someone who knew what her mother was like. All that she had of her dad was the photo. A little colour rectangle of a man wearing incredibly tight trousers, a white shirt, and a thin, thin tie. Derek, July 1979, it said on the back— before she was born.

Stefanie used to look at the picture a lot and wonder where it was taken. Mum said up west, in Regent's Park. But you could never believe what she said. The man in the picture grinned and Stef would hold it up and practise grinning just like Derek. She could get her mouth into exactly the same shape and it was that which had convinced her that he really was her dad, and not just some boyfriend who looked more like Stefanie than any of the others. But that bit wasn't fair. There hadn't been a proper boyfriend since Stefanie was in Year Eight two years ago, so maybe that was Mum's problem.

She heard from Mark that afternoon. Stef had been round at Leona's watching telly and when she got in Mum was sitting in the kitchen with a plastic bag on her head doing her roots.

'You've got a drip.' Stefanie could see a little trail of brown-red hair dye trickling down her mother's neck.

'Thanks, love.'

Stef watched her mum wipe it away then headed for the bathroom. It was as she thought. The sink was stained, and speckles of dye had sprayed up over the mirror and onto the tiles.

'You've done it again, Mum! I have told you.' Stefanie sighed and wound some toilet paper round her hand and started scrubbing at the mess. 'If you don't clean it straight off it just stains.'

There wasn't a lot of point. Even though Stefanie always cleaned up as much as she could there were always old spots from the hundreds of other times Mum had done her hair. 'Covers all grey' it said on the box. Stefanie wiped off as much as she could and picked up the plastic gloves, the little bottles of dye, and the ripped open box. 'Sorrento', it said, 'a rich light auburn', Mum's usual colour. She knew Sorrento was a place because the other colours were all places: Jamaica, Naples, Oslo. Stefanie wondered where Sorrento was and if all the women there had incredibly shiny dark gold hair. Or just all walked around with plastic bags on their heads and dye dripping down their foreheads. Then she tore the box up into little pieces and stuffed it into the pink plastic bathroom bin.

Mum stood in the doorway smiling lamely. 'Sorry, love. I was going to do it.' She unwrapped the plastic bag and rinsed her hair in the sink. Stefanie didn't stop to watch, she knew the sink would look all orange again in five minutes.

In the hall, in the wire basket that collects the letters, was a note. Stefanie thought it was one of those 'phone-a-pizza' things but when she looked closely it had 'Stephanie' written on it in black letters. It was from Mark. 'SEE YOU FRIDAY PHONE US UP MARK' it said in capital letters, like a blackmail note. Underneath was his phone number. Stefanie folded it back in the envelope and took it into her bedroom. Then she unfolded it again and looked at it. He'd written it. Maybe he'd even been round and Mum hadn't noticed, not if she'd had the music up loud. Friday—this Friday. Stefanie folded the note one last time and put it in the box with her photographs. She had to try really hard not to phone him right away.

She held out till Sunday.

4

Stefanie developed and printed the pictures on Monday at school. Technically, it was Camera Club on Tuesday lunchtime. But she had Mr Bartlett like *that* and she could get the keys off him most breaktimes if she wanted. He thought she was responsible. It made her grin just thinking about it. Most of the teachers thought she was just a flake—dim but harmless—not clever enough to be trusted with anything really important. Mrs Roberts their class teacher didn't trust her as far as the office with the register, but here was Bartlett handing over the darkroom keys any time she liked.

The pictures of Amina's family were great. It was the light, Stef thought. Making the brick so contrasty. Making their skin seem darker and their clothes lighter. They all wore glasses—round reflecting discs where their eyes should be. Stef had taken one with the glasses off but they looked like a trio of moles squinting into the sun. Shahid looked good too. Stefanie was pleased. He'd like that. She pegged the pictures up and locked the darkroom behind her. They'd be dry by hometime. Stef grinned. It was going to work—the whole thing was going to look brilliant. So long as she could persuade Mrs Menzies to co-operate. She did have the pictures she hadn't asked about. The ones taken from the balcony. But it wouldn't fit anyway. All the other photos were front on. When she came to putting the photographs all together it would look daft having one from above.

After school Stefanie sorted out the pictures of Amina's family. She kept the two best prints and took the rest, including the ones of Shahid, round to Amina's flat.

Amina answered the door. She was eating a jam sandwich. A huge white fluffy slice of bread oozing scarlet jam. She was still wearing the school uniform, green skirt, white blouse, but Stefanie noticed she'd undone the button on the waistband.

Stefanie waved the pictures at her. 'I've done them. I thought you'd like a look.'

Amina nodded and Stef followed her into the sitting room. The flat was exactly the same way round as Stefanie's. The furniture was different, but the view was almost identical. Shifted slightly, one storey. There was a telly—a big one—flat screen, and a brown table.

Over the gas fireplace were photos: little ones, children, old people, a woman holding a baby.

Amina finished her mouthful. 'They're great.' She was nodding. 'Look at Shahid! What a poser! Are you sure we can have these?'

Stefanie turned round. 'Yeah, 'course. I only need the one.'

'Dad'll be pleased.'

Stefanie picked a photo up off the mantelpiece. 'Is that you?'

It was a woman, a toddler, and a baby in a garden—

33

could've been the rose garden in Victoria Park. The woman smiled contentedly, almost cowlike. Stefanie liked her. You could tell she was kind.

'That's Mum.' Amina pointed with the jam sandwich. Stefanie put the picture down. She knew Amina's mother was dead—an illness, Mum had told her.

'Sorry.'

Amina smiled. 'Don't worry, really.'

'Well, I better be going.' She felt stupid now. Amina might want to chat or something, get the wrong idea.

'Thanks a lot. Really. I'd love to see what you're doing with them.'

'Yeah.' Stefanie headed for the door. 'Sure. Sometime. When I've finished. Maybe.' Stefanie dashed out and ran up the steps to her flat.

5

Mark lived in one of the new houses, almost up against the canal. His dad was on the council and everyone said that was why they were moved in so quickly. The new houses were bright—almost eggy yellow—and so new that the orange wood porches still smelt of wood preservative. The windows were small and square and mean looking, so the house looked as if it was squinting at you. When Stefanie stepped inside she could almost feel the walls pressing in on her, the thick sculpted pile of the carpet smothering her, the still air-freshened air choking her. At home in her flat she could see a bit more sky than this, and the walls seemed slightly further apart. It wasn't perfect—you could always hear the next doors' shouting and that—but it was home.

Mark's mother picked up her magazine, wiping the wooden antique pine effect table top shiny with her sleeve. She even had a gold chain round her neck with 'Mum' on it in case you forgot. She fiddled with the flat gold letters while she looked at Stefanie. Her finger tips and under her nails were silvery black. Lottery fingers, Stef remembered, from the scratchcards. Like when Mum—her mum—would stand in the doorway with the shopping. Holding the card like a golden ticket. As if she would have more chance of winning half in and half out. Scratching with her pink varnished nails; you could see the anticipation build in her face.

'I don't want much, love,' she'd say. 'A grand or two or ten would be nice.' Then the smile would fade and Mum's face would crumple ever so slightly, and the scratchcard ended up stuffed behind the heater in the hall.

'I don't know why you buy those things, Mum.' Stef always said that but she'd bought one herself, more than once.

'Tea, love?' Mark's mother sounded hopeful. She got up, patting her straight hair smooth and headed for the kitchen.

Stefanie opened her mouth but Mark beat her to it.

' 'S all right, Mum, we're off.'

'You sure, love?'

Mark said nothing and checked his hair in the mirror.

Stef smiled at his mum to say sorry, but Mark was already at the door.

'Are we off then or what?' he called.

Stef got up. She'd put new shoes on and they were killing her but she smiled. Until you've done the heavy stuff it's all smiles, she thought. Once, a boy she'd met on holiday sent her a letter. 'Your lips suck forth my soul.' She passed it round in Fabric Crafts. Stef thought he'd made it up. For her. Then Leona showed her it written down in a book. It was made up four hundred years ago. Give or take.

Outside the air was thick with aphids.

'Where are we going?' Stef tried to sound easy.

'The basin,' he said.

Stef didn't think the basin was such a good idea for snogging but she said nothing. There was building round the basin now, luxury homes, waterside developments, that kind of thing. Stef had tried to imagine living in a place like that, standing over a sink full of washing up and looking out at Rotherhithe across the greasy river. That was not her idea of luxury.

Mark walked ahead of her to the canal. The water was red with the sunset and buzzing with flies. Stef tried not to think of raw meat. She smiled. Why did she want to smile? A vision of one of Becky's collection of grinning plastic trolls popped up into her mind. She squashed it down again quick and tried to think cool instead. It was hard. So hard that she decided to concentrate on the way her toes were squeezed and pinched in the new shoes, and made her take little scrunched up pigeon steps. It didn't help that the towpath was gravelly and pitted.

The canal opened out into the basin. It was so different now, just the shape of the water had stayed the same. There were some half built flats on one side—builders had gone bust, Mark said. They'd been unfinished for years. Warehouse-style apartments—said a sign—private gym and sauna. Completion 2001. New York Loft Living. The sign had been up so long the paint hung off in strips.

Mark started across the canal walking along the top of the lock gates and Stefanie wished she'd worn trainers, or at least the scuffed-up black loafers she wore for school sometimes. He held out his hand to her and she inched across, staring down into the water thick with plastic bottles, bags, every kind of rubbish. Still, if she fell in she'd most likely not sink through all the crap but she shut her lips tight in case she slipped.

He half lifted her off. Both his hands were inside her

jacket—squeezing her tight—almost in her armpits. She felt her heart going and smiled at him. She wanted him to kiss her right now, right here. She stared at him hoping he'd read her mind, but he walked on. Maybe he didn't want to kiss. Maybe she had got it wrong. She couldn't ask him, couldn't say, 'Give us a snog'. Girls only do that kind of stuff in *J-17*, she thought.

'Did you go to that thing? That thing up the park?' He spoke. Stefanie felt so relieved. It was going to be all right. He didn't look round though and Stefanie quickened to catch up with him.

'What, on Globetown Fields?' Stefanie shrugged. 'I never. I was doing my photos.'

'You should've come.'

'You never asked.' Stefanie tried looking alluringly at him and hoped none of her lipstick had come off onto her teeth. It was that new orangey one of Beck's from Miss Selfridge but it was a bit greasy.

'I mean you should've come with your camera.'

'Oh.'

'Yeah. There was some major trouble. Some boys from Shadwell school got hold of one of ours . . . '

'Our what?' Stef was lost. 'I thought you'd left school?'

'Yeah, but if you think I'm going to stand there while some no-brain from Shadwell beats my mates up . . . You know.' Stefanie didn't, but she nodded anyway. 'That Shadwell lot are really in for it. Thinking they can get away with acting like that, on our patch, Globetown Fields.' He shook his head and sat down on a bench.

Stefanie tried to imagine how she was going to tell Becky about this at school. She sat down next to him.

'Did he kiss you and that, then?' Beck would go and Stef would say, 'No. But I nearly fell in the canal and he told me all about some really big fight and then we went home.' Stefanie tried not to look too bored. Talk to him, she said to herself. Listen to him, that's what it says in the girls' comics. Listen, and stare into his eyes and then at his lips. She stared.

Eyes, lips. Lips, eyes. Maybe she was being too obvious—try it slower. Eyes . . . Lips. Perhaps that time he kissed her was a dream or something, perhaps it never happened and Stefanie had made it all up. She thought she would burst but Mark didn't seem to notice anything at all.

'Shit!' He felt his pockets, patting them. 'I've forgotten my fags.'

Stefanie kissed him. They kissed for ages until Stefanie felt her neck seizing up and pulled away. Mark's mouth was Amber Flame. Stefanie tried rubbing it off with her fingers.

'Sorry.'

Mark took her hand and smiled. 'We better find a shop that sells fags then.'

'I don't smoke,' Stef said.

They had to go back across the canal. On a balcony above them a young woman was sitting drinking coffee, reading a book. The Limehouse Link motorway rumbled to the south of them.

'Look at that daft yuppie cow.' Mark pointed up at her. The woman didn't notice anything. 'Where does she think she is?'

Stefanie was terrified he was going to start shouting up at the woman. So she was relieved when they walked out of the basin under the railway bridge.

'Do you know where you're going?' Stefanie asked. It wasn't that they were lost, it was just that Stefanie knew they were on the edge of the White Horse estate, and the White Horse was all Shadwell. Mark must know that, she thought. Mark had only left school a year ago.

The White Horse estate was huge; big red brick low rises each with a curving nineteen thirties arch, like a yawning mouth, that opened onto a central courtyard lined with balconies.

You went through one of those arches uninvited and you were walking dead. Becky said that's what her brother said and he should know. Once, she said, Martin and his mate Dean had chased this boy. He ran flat out from as far as the railway. They almost had him, she said. Pulled his blazer but he ran out of it, and before they knew it they were at the White Horse and he ran right in and Marty and Dean just followed. Then all of a sudden, Beck says, the balconies were lined with boys all looking down at Martin and Dean. All just looking and it's all quiet and Marty can hear his heart under his school shirt. Thumping real hard, like it would explode, and no one says nothing, they just look. And the boy they were chasing is smiling— grinning at them. Then this one boy standing up on the first balcony pulls out a spanner, a massive heavy shiny one, and he's banging it down in his hand like baddies do on the telly. Martin thought he'd shat himself and him and Dean just ran. Ran all the way home.

Mark pushed the door of the newsagent's open, but Stefanie stayed outside. She tried to look in to the estate through the nearest arch. It looked like the car park under her block, familiar, ordinary: a couple of cars, a couple of kids messing about. Little kids, not big scary ones. Little girls clacking along in too big mummy's shoes. Sandals with flashes of gold and stuck on plastic jewels. Running in and out of the cars in bright coloured shiny party frocks, some not done up properly, some sweeping the ground. Shrieking and yelling, almost in English. Pink and gold and gauzy blue.

The light was good too—heavy and yellow and slanting into the car park. It looked nothing like the instant arena of death that Becky went on about. When London looked like this Stef knew she never wanted to leave. It made her forget about the cockroaches and all the crap, it just made her feel warm. Stefanie wished she'd brought the camera. She imagined the scene framed and flattened. Cropped a bit—less ground and more sky. Black and whitened. Matt paper. Nice. Mark stepped out of the newsagent's.

'You're staring.'

'Yeah, it's the light.' Stefanie's stomach hit the floor. Why did she always go and open her mouth before thinking. She sounded like some mental hippy. What a stupid hippy thing to say. She felt her cheeks go hot and prickly.

'What?' Maybe he'd misheard her. He stood next to where Stef was standing, looked where she was looking. Moved his head around to make sure.

'Nothing. I mean I was just looking. For a photo, maybe.' Stef turned the other way so he couldn't see her pink face and looked interested in the new spiky church on the other side of the road.

'It's the White Horse, innit,' Mark said, still looking. 'Pile of crap. Used to be all right till they moved that lot in.'

Stefanie knew exactly what he meant, but wondered if he could remember a time when the East End was white. If he could remember a time when the White Horse was where anyone wanted to live. Stefanie felt sure that if you asked, no one would want to live there. What Stefanie wondered was why they weren't knocking down the White Horse instead of all-white or mixed estates like hers. She opened her mouth to say something then shut it again. What was the point. She couldn't change how he thought. Mark plopped the packet of cigs in his pocket and started walking. Stefanie found herself smiling at him and they walked back to the basin to snog a bit more.

When Stefanie got home the big toes on both feet were red and livid and hot like the ring on the electric cooker turned up to five. She stuck her feet in a bowl of cold water and checked it wasn't too late to phone Becky.

6

It wasn't long before going out with Mark was something she did every weekend. Mark had taken her to a couple of clubs, but Stefanie didn't look much more than fifteen, so now they went to the cinema instead. It was a routine; school all week, film with Mark on Saturday, round to Mark's on a Sunday to play tapes or to watch Mark and his mates play video games. That was really boring. 'Sitting around being decorative' Mum called it, and Stef shuddered 'cause she knew it was almost true. She would end up having to talk to Danielle who went out with Lee and was totally brain dead. She knew she should be doing stuff for her model—with the photos—especially now she'd taken them all.

It made her feel stupid. Sitting on the edge of the bed while the boys played football for hours. Stupid like Danielle. Sometimes she wondered if Mark thought she and Danielle were the same just because they were girls.

It also made her feel really guilty, and scared. Because

maybe Mum was right, maybe the photography was like the ice skating. Maybe in a year from now the photos would be sitting in their flat 10 × 8 box in the bottom of her wardrobe with the white boots. Maybe all she'd care about was how she looked walking through Victoria Park of a Saturday with Mark. It made her cold.

She liked the cinema though, that was good. She liked sitting in the dark and she liked the films. So big—right there up in front of you. And she liked the way films skipped all the boring bits of life. Like moving photos. You could frame the shots just the way you wanted—leave out all the crap. She liked the lighting and the reaction shots and the way one picture was cut right up against another to take your breath away. That was what she wanted out of her model, out of her photos. Ordinary people—not film stars with make-up and that. But ordinary people—who you could look at and get something from just by looking. It was so hard to explain. She had tried explaining it to Mark but she could see him switching off and she knew it was pointless. 'You'll see,' she said sometimes and hoped she was right.

They usually kissed through all the adverts and she had to stop him touching her during the film, because then she couldn't concentrate. Not that she didn't like it some of the time but not if it was a really good film.

Afterwards they usually walked home along the Mile End Road and one time when Stef had her camera, she took Mark's picture. She took it in front of the old jeweller's with the big curving windows and black and gold paint. It had a mosaicky floor with 'Schallers' set into it in swooping letters. Nan said all the shops on the Mile End Road had been as smart as that once. Stef had taken a few—one straight on—dead boring, Stef thought. Mark trying to look cool and interesting leaning on the curve of the glass. Another of him walking past the windows and a third taken through the bulge of glass. In the viewfinder Mark's head had been distorted. Smudged, like a fairground mirror reflection.

'Open your mouth a bit more, and turn your head,' Stef had called.

'Like this?' The curvy glass pulled his face around.

'Yeah, that's weird, that is.' The camera clicked and lit up the street for a second with the flash.

One thing about Mark, he did like having his picture taken. Him and his mates hanging around. They always wanted to look dead tough and that in the pictures, but they always ended up looking like little boys being stupid. Once Mark had seen one of her books—a book of photos that Bartlett had lent her. Portraits of tramps and that—down and outs. 'Why does anyone want to take pictures of them?' he'd said. Sometimes Stefanie didn't know why she went out with him. He liked one in the other book of the Kray twins in their suits, though. 'Do one like that, Stef, me and Gavin and Lee. Yeah, go on.' He kissed her. 'Go on, I'll grease me hair down like that,' he posed staring at her, curling his lip very slightly. 'Go on, Stefanie.'

So she did on a Saturday—a week or so later—in the little road of old houses this side of the canal. It was all artists living here, Becky said. Posh, she said. She'd seen it on the telly. It was an artists' colony and they spent all day making chocolate fountains, or painting crap paintings that looked like nothing. Becky said that East London had more artists living in it than any other city in Europe. But no one believed her. If that was true, Stef said, why didn't they make the place look a bit better? The street looked just like *Coronation Street*. Tiny houses built right onto the pavement and a dark brick railway bridge cut the road in half. Just like London when the Krays lived, Lee said. Gavin said he was stupid and they were still alive. Then

Becky who had come to watch said one was still alive and the other wasn't but she couldn't remember which and they went on and on.

Stefanie had to shut them up so she could get on with the photographs. None of the boys wore suits, and there were three of them, so Stefanie had no idea what they expected.

'It's going to look nothing like that other picture, you know,' Stef said.

'Pure gangsta style,' Lee said, grinning.

They'd all done their hair and Mark said they should all be shaking hands, and looking hard. Becky whispered that they looked like they were doing some sort of grumpy country dancing all standing together scowling and Stef had to hold her breath to stop herself giggling.

Stefanie got them to stand in the middle of the road and looked up at them. She didn't know if they'd like it.

'I'm wasted on you lot, honest I am,' she said.

'Too bloody true,' Becky said under her breath.

Mark's bedroom had black wallpaper with red and grey stripes and a matching duvet set. He had an Arsenal sticker on the window and big posters of that woman off the TV with the breast implants, in a swimsuit. Stefanie thought that if she bought a wonderbra she could get her tits to look like that—well, a bit. But they were nearly twenty quid in that shop in the Roman Road. Less in the market, but Becky had one and it never seemed to do much for her. Becky was flat as a table anyway. Becky's mum didn't like it. She said it was criminal what girls— so young—did nowadays. But Becky had bought it with her birthday money and hidden it in her drawer. Stef had tried it on but she was a 34C and Beck 32AA. More like 32AAAAAAAAGGHHH, Beck said.

Mark said she had nice tits and just thinking about him saying that, and touching her, made Stef feel really good, even if she was just walking along to school or getting the tea, or something. If she was doing something really boring, she could just forget she was there by thinking about him. That's what convinced her she wanted to do it with him.

Becky said as soon as you do it with them then they're just not interested any more. And she should know because she'd had more boyfriends than Stef and she had actually done it, with Gavin. And anyway, she said, doing it wasn't that great. She preferred all the kissing stuff and you don't have to worry about getting pregnant or Aids or their hipbones bumping into you.

Stefanie knew she was going to do it with Mark. She never said so out loud, even to Becky. But specially not to Mark. He'd think she was some kind of slag. No, she'd make him think he'd persuaded her. But she had decided she was going to do it with Mark and soon, in case she changed her mind. Anyway—like Becky said—it wasn't such a big deal. Stefanie had said no once. Just so that Mark would know she was a nice girl; but now, right now was perfect.

Mark's parents had gone to some big shopping centre in Essex and wouldn't be back for ages. It was sunny outside and it felt strange being daytime. Stefanie had always imagined doing it in the dark. It would have been much easier because this spot had come up on her back and her legs were really nasty, she thought. Like plucked raw chicken skin. But if she kept them under the duvet he'd never notice. She had imagined taking all her clothes off and getting into his bed. Lying there waiting for him. But that was a bit dramatic.

Stefanie had taken a couple of condoms out of Mum's knicker drawer. She knew Mum'd never notice. The packet was right at the back—it had been there for years. She'd even taken one out to show to Becky once in Year

Seven. Stefanie sat down on Mark's bed. She thought that if he took too long she might go right off the idea. Then her stomach turned over. What if the condoms were out of date. What if they split or just fell apart 'cause they were so old? Maybe she should open one to check? Maybe she should do that now, but then what if there was anything wrong with the other one? She pulled up the stripy curtain a tiny bit and saw Mark coming back from the video shop. It was too late—she'd just have to risk it. Stef looked up at silicone woman on the wall, and touched them for luck. Or something.

Afterwards she wanted Mark to do it again, but the other condom was dodgy and although Mark swore he had some, by the time he'd gone through all the drawers in the house Stefanie wanted to put her clothes on again in case his mum and dad came home.

Stefanie felt almost totally happy. She could still feel him where he'd been next to her and smell the wonderful smell of his skin. She felt so good she wanted to go home and finish her pictures and be nice to Mrs Menzies, even to Mum.

'I'll see you later.' Mark kissed her in the hall.

'Yeah, later.' Stefanie heard his parents' car pull up in the carport outside.

'Afternoon, Mrs Brody.' She smiled at Mark's mother, unloading a new Hoover and pedal bin. Stefanie grinned. What she wanted to say—what she wanted to shout—was, 'I've just shagged your son, Mrs Brody. Just now, upstairs, in your house.'

'Lovely day, Stefanie.' Mr Brody locked the car door. He had a moustache and Stefanie couldn't help thinking how horrible it must be to kiss him. I wonder if they can tell? Stef thought. If I look different? She checked her reflection in the Sainsbury's up by the market. Then she laughed at herself for being so daft and ran the rest of the way home.

7

Becky's birthday was the first Friday in July. Stefanie knew she had wanted a party—a real party with no parents—but with Becky's parents that was never going to happen. Becky said her mum had said only twenty people and everyone home by midnight. Becky had said that was just too embarrassing and what did they think anyway, she was fifteen. But she didn't get the party. What she got was an evening out with Stef and Leona. Not even up west, just to the Multiplex on the Isle of Dogs. Miles away, Stef had said under her breath. But Becky said it was really good—they had everything there and the bus from Mile End went all the way.

Stefanie had bought a little skirt up the Roman Road two weeks ago. She hadn't worn it yet, not out anyway. She had put it on tons of times and stood in front of the mirror. Tried on every single top she had and some of Mum's. But she didn't think Mark would like it. She didn't have to think about Mark tonight. She did her

mascara—and had a go with the red lipstick
ed from Leona.

m out.' Normally Mum said nothing. Never
the telly, but tonight she was standing in
tween her and the door. Stefanie's heart sank.
She did not want to be told her hair would be better
another way or that her clothes weren't right. Mum
smiled.

'Where are you going, love?'

Stefanie couldn't believe it. 'Becky's birthday. I told
you over and over.' Stefanie couldn't believe how dim her
mother could be sometimes.

'Don't be like that. I do worry. You know I do, love.'
She stood close and smoothed a bit of Stefanie's hair
down. Stefanie thought she must have been watching a
slushy movie to have gone all maternal like this. This was
almost the mother she wanted. But not right now.

'I'm just out with Becky and Leona. I'll be late.'

Mum sighed and looked at her soppily. 'Oh, Steffie.
You look so grown up. Fifteen.' Mum said the last word
like a long breath.

'Mum!' Stefanie pulled on her jacket.

'Tell you what—tell you what, love. Just let me do your
face. You'd like that. I haven't done that for ages! Come
on, it won't take a minute.'

Stefanie sighed. 'I'm late, Mum.' But she couldn't
refuse. 'Only if you're really, really quick.'

Mum ushered her into her bedroom and sat her at the
dressing table. Mum had more make-up than the local
chemist: cream shadow, powder shadow, pencils and
crayons. Stefanie reckoned she must have nicked half of
it, but then some of it was that old. She even had old
fashioned blocks of mascara and huge long false eyelashes
like insect legs. She had loads of brushes too, of every
thickness. And hundreds and hundreds of lipsticks, some

worn right down, but she still kept them, brushing the last bits of colour up out of the tube.

Mum looked at Stefanie in the mirror and smiled. 'I'll be quick, love.' When Stef was little she had played at make-up with Mum. Spending hours having her nails painted and her hair done. Just like Mummy. But it had got boring and stupid and Stefanie had said so and Mum hadn't offered to do her face for ages. Mum could be quite good. As long as she didn't go over the top with foundation and blusher and dark brown lip liner she'd be OK. Anything for a quiet life, Stef thought.

'I don't want that foundation, Mum, please. Just eyes and mouth.'

She hoped Mum took that in. 'Just close your eyes now, love, that's it.' And she wiped the mascara and liner that Stefanie had just put on right off. 'You're going to be beautiful.' Stefanie sighed and tried to think of nothing. It was quite a nice feeling. The brushes gently fanning her face. Mum hovering round her, taking time, concentrating. Almost too good to be true.

In fifteen minutes Stefanie was done.

'What do you think?' Mum stood behind her talking to Stef's reflection. Stefanie couldn't believe it. Mum had actually done what she was told.

'Mum, that's brilliant, really.' Mum was standing behind her smiling into the mirror.

'Yeah, I used brown mascara instead of your black. It's too hard with your colouring, but you never listen.'

Stefanie smiled. She felt like the 'after' photo of some dreggy girl in a magazine. Smiling and beautiful and new.

'Thanks, Mum, thanks.' Stefanie went to kiss Mum on the cheek but she pulled away.

'Don't want to spoil your face, love. You make sure you have a lovely time.' Mum turned away behind the door and Stef took the camera from the hook in the hall and dashed out. She had reached the bottom of the stairs when the music started up.

Stefanie stopped, half meaning to run back and try and make it all right, when she realized she should have been at Becky's half an hour ago. What was Mum doing? Stefanie couldn't work it out, but it seemed to be getting worse. Summer comes and Mum goes loopy. It had been like that for at least three years. But this year it seemed worse.

They were waiting at Becky's. Leona in a pair of short white shorts and Becky in some outfit she'd got for her birthday.

'Happy birthday, Beck.' Stefanie handed her the photo. It was Becky close up—big face. 'It's that time in the park . . . you were singing, remember?'

Becky grinned, 'I'm not going to forget now, am I? It's lovely, Stef, thanks.'

Becky's mum had bought her a gold chain and a pair of proper loafers from that shop in the West End. 'Real designer they are,' Becky said, and Stefanie and Leona were impressed.

'Be good girls.' Becky's mum watched them go. 'Me and your dad are at your Aunty Elaine's, but don't hang around anywhere and come straight home. We'll be back for half eleven and I expect you to be.'

'Yes, Mum.'

The bus took ages to get to the island. When they finally got to the cinema the film they wanted to see had started so they hung around in the foyer drinking those massive paper cups full of Coke and seeing who could burp loudest. Becky was eating prawn cocktail crisps so hers smelt the worst.

'How old are we meant to be?' Stef was killing herself.

Stefanie was taking some photos of Becky and Leona

pretending to look sophisticated when Becky stopped suddenly. 'Check that boy over there, there look!' Becky pointed with her paper cup. 'Don't look now!' But they did. 'Tasty or what?' and Becky grinned at him over the edge of her drink like in an advert.

'We don't know you, OK?' Stefanie and Leona backed away laughing. It never took Becky long to sort anything and ten minutes later the girls were out of the cinema, walking off the island through the orange lit tunnel that went under the motorway.

Leona was nervous. 'Your mum'll kill you.' They were walking just behind the boy from the cinema, Nathan, and his mate.

'There's a party,' Becky had said. 'Up Poplar.' She was smiling. They'd missed the film and Becky said it would be a laugh. And it was her birthday after all.

'We don't even know them!' Leona said—not too loud in case the boys heard. 'You're mad, you are.' She was feeling cold in her shorts. Stefanie knew really that Leona was right, but they had the cinema money for a taxi if anything went wrong.

'Come on, Le,' Stef said, 'give it a go.'

'Yeah, come on, Leona,' Becky said. 'Leona the moaner. You just might have some fun.'

Stefanie knew she was the only one of the three of them who wouldn't get killed. Mum would never know so she supposed it didn't matter.

Leona moaned all the way to the dirty brick low rise estate where the boys stopped. 'Can't be much of a party. You can't even hear any music.'

She was right. The party was crap. It was in a flat near the flyover that went down to the tunnel under the Thames. Stefanie pulled her jacket tighter. Now it was really night, it felt cold. The flat smelt of dog and Stefanie counted eleven people including the couple snogging in the hall. The front room had wallpaper with giant pink flowers but Stef couldn't be sure as the only light was a table lamp with an orange bulb stuck in it. On the shelf above the gas fire were pictures of three children all grinning, standing one behind the other. There was a low black table with a bowl of Twiglets and a huge fish tank, lit up and bubbling, full of tiny little fish with flashes of electric blue along their backs. Neons, Stef remembered from *Blue Peter* or some kids' show.

'It looks more exciting in there,' Stef said, looking into the fish tank.

Leona wanted to go straight away but Becky said she was sure it would liven up and went off with Nathan into the kitchen. Stef sat down next to Leona on the sofa. Becky came back with three bottles of fizzy pink sweet stuff. 'Wine,' she said. Stef couldn't really taste it was pink, but she read it off the label. Becky said Nathan said it was still early. Leona said if there wasn't any dancing soon she was off, and Becky said what's stopping you? Leona said she wasn't getting up to dance round in someone's living room with a couple of lads sitting there watching and a poxy little CD player and no proper system. Becky just shrugged.

'It's my birthday,' she said, 'and I'm having fun.' And she turned the CD up and started really going for it. 'You can take my picture if you like.'

Stefanie pulled her skirt down. Suddenly a short skirt didn't seem like such a good idea. She wished they were back in the cinema in the dark in one of those big seats with holders for your popcorn. She wished she'd gone out with Mark. Or better still stayed in with him. Leona started going through the pile of CDs and tapes, then gave up and sat next to Stef again. Stefanie sipped her pink drink in quick little gulps so she didn't actually taste it and it just slipped down into her tummy making a warm feeling.

Stef wished she could dance like Becky. Dance and not care. Just dance.

The boy who wasn't Nathan sat on the edge of the sofa next to her and Stef inched slowly nearer Leona. 'What's the matter with you two?' he said.

'Nothing's the matter. We're just overcome with excitement.' Stefanie didn't even bother to look at him.

'Let's go, Stef.' Leona wriggled her arms back into the sleeves of her jacket. 'Come on. If Becky wants to get off with that Nathan she doesn't need us.'

'But we can't just leave her!'

'I'm phoning for a cab. If I'm not back soon I'll have to explain why I wasn't where I said I was, and this "party" is not worth any grief from my dad.'

Becky was dancing close with Nathan now, touching almost all the way down their bodies. Stefanie knew she would have trouble getting Becky out of here. Maybe she should leave her.

Leona came back from the phone. 'Ten minutes, they said. Did you tell Becky?'

'You try telling her.' Becky and Nathan were kissing now. 'You couldn't get a knife between them.'

'I'm going to wait outside.' Leona stood up and grabbed a handful of Twiglets before heading for the door. Stefanie got up too.

'Becky.' She had to shout. 'Beck.' Becky disengaged, smiling. 'Becky, we're going.'

Nathan was still holding her, running his hands under her top. Then suddenly Becky lurched sideways and sort of slid out of his hold and was on the floor at Stef's feet. Stef's first thought was that it was drugs—like off the telly where some boy spikes your drink. But then there was another girl standing in the space where Becky had been.

She was shouting at Nathan. Smacking him round the face.

Stefanie helped Becky up. She was all right, she said. Her face hurt, she said. Nathan was holding the other girl's hands—like you would a child to stop it hitting you. They were shouting. Her name was Tasha, Natasha maybe.

'Come on, Beck, let's go.' Stef kept it quiet. They could get out now and wait for the cab and be home in no time.

Becky was furious—Stef could see that. 'Come on, Beck, leave it.' Stefanie held her arm. Led her out of the room towards the front door. Stefanie could see it up ahead. They would get out and it would be all right.

Then Becky turned back, Stefanie just behind her, just in time to see Becky punch the other girl hard in the stomach. Hard enough to make her double up and fall sideways.

'No one hits me,' Becky said, glaring at Natasha like she was ready to get her again if she got up. Natasha tried heaving herself up on the black table, pulling the fish tank over, releasing a small-scale tidal wave and hundreds of tiny fluorescent fish out over the carpet.

Becky grinned and ran. Stef followed. 'You bloody idiot, Beck!' And they sped down the stairs to the street.

Becky was laughing like a mad woman. Stefanie felt a little bit scared. They ran out of the entrance to the block just in time to see Leona in her cab heading for home.

They had to walk. Becky had £6.37 and a phone card, but they couldn't find a box that worked and anyway within ten minutes they were halfway home.

'I should have got Dad to get me a mobile for my birthday instead of these shoes.' They got some chips from a Chinese that was still open and decided to save their cab money and walk. There were two of them, Becky said, and they could run if they had to. Stefanie was happy.

She could spend her taxi money on card to frame her photographs. She linked arms with Becky.

'Great birthday, innit?'

They would have been quicker just following the canal. Walking up the towpath until Mile End, but Stefanie said it would be safer on the road. 'Some nutter could come up behind you and push you in, and you'd never know till it's too late.'

Becky agreed and they kept walking. It was the best bit, Stef thought. Walking down the streets in your town not caring. It felt like no one could get them. Becky would just kick them in the balls and they'd laugh. They were kerb-crawled a couple of times by sick old men but they both laughed and swore at them. Stefanie liked feeling this brave.

They turned north before the railway. They weren't mad enough to waltz into the White Horse. Neither girl said anything, it was just obvious. Becky was singing really loudly and Stef had given up trying to shush her. Her voice was bouncing off the brick of the railway viaduct and seemed huge in the quiet dark. 'Want some of your brown sugar,' she went, even louder so her voice started cracking. Beck stepped over the knee-high railing that fenced off a patch of grass just by the bridge.

'Watch out for the dog shit,' Stef called.

'I'm not watching. I'm singing,' Becky said. 'You can look for me,' and she started up again. Stef jumped over too. She didn't want to be too far away from Becky, just in case.

Becky stopped. 'Oh my God, Stef! Oh my God! There's someone here.' Becky felt the body with the toe of her West End loafer. Stefanie ran up.

'Is it dead? My God, Stef!'

Stefanie saw the T-shirt and knelt down. She had seen

the T-shirt before. Becky turned him over gently with her foot. It was Shahid. Amina's brother.

In the yellow street light Shahid looked tender and bloody as a Saturday night steak. His nose seemed to have smudged sideways over his left cheek. He was covered with shiny globs of blood or phlegm like little red slugs. His T-shirt—the white one in the photo—was darkened with air-brush sprays of blood. Stef stared. She couldn't stop. She couldn't look away.

'Beck, Beck.' She said it in a normal voice but she had meant to yell. 'Get an ambulance! Get one now!' Stefanie heard Becky turn and run. Stef stood still, half bent over Shahid's body, unable to step forwards or backwards. Inside her head Miss Tunnadine, Humanities, was doing the first aid talk. Stef imagined herself bending forwards, listening for his heart, gently curling Shahid into the recovery position. But she couldn't bear to touch him.

She felt for the camera and without taking her eyes off Shahid she flipped it out of its case and lifted it to her face. Through the rectangle of the viewfinder Shahid looked acceptable—flatter—his face not quite so swollen, the blood less red and shiny. She pressed the shutter. She knew she shouldn't. The heavy chunk click sounded too loud. The flash lit up his face and it looked grey. It didn't wake him, he never moved, he didn't even groan, like beaten up people usually do on the telly. She took one more picture in case then shut the camera away and hid it inside her coat.

Before she knew it Becky was back and some people had come out from the houses over the road to have a look.

'Is he dead?'

'Dunno.'

'Is he breathing though, is he?'

Becky put her hand a centimetre away from his lips. Huge and swollen and shiny like curling slabs of meat.

'Don't!' Stefanie shouted. Pulling her friend's hand away and jumping back. Then about a dozen sirens all sounded at once and there was an ambulance crew and the girls watched as the ambulance people buzzed round him. Getting out a stretcher and loading him up.

Couldn't be dead, Beck said, 'cause they never covered him with a sheet and they always do that if they're dead. They did do that electric shock thing with the pads that made Shahid's body jerk about and they did inject him with something. But Beck was sure he wasn't dead.

Stefanie hoped so. She'd never meant to take pictures of someone dead. Maybe she should open the camera and rip the film right out. She shook her head. Becky tugged at her and they slipped away. Running without stopping to Becky's house in case the police asked them anything.

The estate was quiet. The traffic sounded far away and the trees were moving in the wind. The houses were dark. The girls stopped running and sat down on the wall outside Becky's house.

'You go in, Beck,' Stefanie said when she'd caught her breath. 'I'll be OK.'

'Not much of a birthday!' Becky said prising off her loafers. 'Good fight though! Did you see that girl's face when I whopped her!'

Stefanie had forgotten about the party. She was thinking about Shahid. 'I just hope he's not dead,' Stefanie said. 'I wonder who whopped him?'

'He won't be dead. He's too young.' Becky was sure and that made Stef feel better. She smiled.

'I'll ring you tomorrow then,' Becky said. Stef nodded.

Suddenly behind them the porch light clicked on and Becky's mother was standing in the doorway in a full length dressing gown and fluffy slippers.

'Rebecca, where have you been!' Her voice hovered between tears and anger.

'Well I'm back now, so it's all right.'

Stefanie could tell Becky was about to get it so she stood up.

'Bye, Mrs Oliver—Becky.' Stefanie started walking.

'Where do you think you're going, my girl?' Mrs Oliver had learnt a lot about shouting from the teachers she'd been working with. She managed to make her voice low yet threatening. Stefanie stopped dead. 'Don't think you can just walk away into the night! It may be all right with *your* mother, but it is definitely not all right with me!'

Stefanie was angry; she opened her mouth but nothing came out. Mrs Oliver made Stefanie wait for a lift from Becky's dad. She sat in the kitchen while they had a go at Becky in the front room. Stefanie looked at her face distorted in the chrome trim on the cooker. The fridge was covered with magnets and little notes. Martin Football Thursday. Becky INSET day July 4th. Dentist and doctor's appointments. Normal stuff. Stefanie felt weepy and swallowed. The front room went quiet and Stefanie heard Becky's loafer-less feet thump upstairs.

Becky's dad had put a jacket on over his pyjamas. He looked more tired than cross. Stefanie walked with him to the garage and he drove her home in silence. Stefanie concentrated on the flickery red lights on the dashboard display.

It was one o'clock on the kitchen clock when Stef got in. The light in the front room was on and Mum was playing Aretha: 'Darling you-ou send me, Darling you-ou send me, honest you do.' She didn't bother yelling at her. Didn't say anything. Stef stood in the doorway to the front room and watched Mum swaying, saying nothing. Stefanie sat down on her bed and wept.

8

Stefanie woke up still in her clothes from last night. They were hard and sweaty on her like damp cardboard. The light was strong and yellow—sickly almost—and it was hot already. She looked at her alarm clock, six-thirty. Stefanie undressed and bathed and went back to lie in bed, but she couldn't sleep. When she shut her eyes Shahid was there, red and bloody asking her how the photos looked. She flicked the radio on. It was still only eight.

At half-past she got up and put the kettle on and sat in the kitchen with the window open. Downstairs the cats were calling for Mrs Menzies to feed them and a couple of little kids were trundling round the car park on their bikes ringing their bells. Stefanie felt sure she could hear a blackbird singing. She was listening really hard, trying to concentrate. Everything sounded different without the background noise of the building work— sharper, more brittle.

She thought about Amina in the flat below. If she was

asleep—if she knew yet. But maybe she was at the hospital next to his bed and Shahid was sitting up laughing through his swollen lips. But what if she hadn't seen him at all? What if Shahid was already dead? What if she had a dead boy's photograph in the camera?

The door bell went. Stefanie almost dropped the mug of tea. She drew her dressing gown tighter and went into the hall. She looked across into Mum's bedroom. She was still asleep, dead to the world, mouth open, sprawled face down on her bed like a dead body. Stefanie pulled the bedroom door shut as she passed and stood still for a moment. Stood dead quiet behind the front door trying to look through the spy hole. But she couldn't see anything. She wished whoever it was would go away. Then the bell rang again. Really loud this time—because Stefanie was standing right next to the white plastic box where the noise came out. She opened the door instantly and then Mark was there pushing against the door chain.

'What are you doing?' Stef asked.

It isn't even nine yet, Stef thought. She unhooked the door chain. Mark seemed nervous—in a hurry.

'Get me in!' He was carrying a fishing bag and a couple of rods. Stefanie looked at him.

'Night fishing, innit. I've been up all night with Gavin.'

'Lucky Gavin.'

Stefanie was suddenly aware that Mark had never been in the flat before. She'd always persuaded him to wait outside or pick her up on the corner outside the car park. Suddenly she was terrified Mum would wake up and start talking to him. Smiling at him over her morning tea, making eyes at him. Being embarrassing.

'Keep it down,' she whispered. 'Mum's still asleep.' Then she led him into her bedroom. Stefanie managed to shove the dirty clothes from last night under the duvet and kick a box of tampons under the bed. She opened the window wider and flipped off her slippers. Maybe then he would think she was relaxed. Mark wasn't. He sat on the bed picking at the cuticles on his thumb. Nibbling bits off and almost twitching. Stefanie thought he looked like Danny Whitmore after she'd caught him opening the school camera and filling it with the tiny little men from his Galaxy Wars micro world.

'It's serious.' Mark didn't look up. 'That Asian. That one last night.'

Stef nodded. She knew who he meant.

'You saw him, didn't you? You and Becky. You were there.'

'Yeah, last night.' Stefanie shivered. 'He looked like raw meat.'

Mark glanced up at her just for a second. 'Did you see anyone—anyone else?'

'Like who?'

'Did you see it happen?'

'No.' She shook her head. 'He was just lying there. Horrible.' Stefanie watched Mark. He'd pulled a thin, thin strip of skin right down from the bottom of his thumb nail almost to the first joint. At the top it made a V shape, reddening then filling up with blood. Stefanie had never really noticed his hands before. 'You shouldn't bite them, you know.'

Mark hid his fingers in fists. 'Did he . . . did he say something?' Mark wasn't looking at her.

'What is this?' Stefanie felt strange. Was it Mark's boots and hands that had laid into Shahid? Blown his face up, cut the skin on his cheek? She breathed in too fast and felt dizzy. Felt as if she was there again on that bit of land by the railway and Mark was tearing into Shahid. Tearing into any bloody Paki that came along. Any Shadwell Paki. She held on to the window ledge and forced herself to breathe slower. Slower and slower until the pumping noise had stopped inside her head.

Mark had pulled one of her tissues out from the box by her bed and wrapped it round his thumb. But the blood had started coming through anyway. Spreading in a red-on-white flower shape.

'Was it you, then? Was it?'

Mark laughed. 'Don't be daft.'

He's laughing 'cause he's guilty. Stefanie shook the thought out of her head. She had kissed him, she thought. Kissed him practically everywhere, let him do anything. Someone who could turn a human person into bloody meat. She stared at the shape of his mouth. She knew exactly how the colour of his lips changed when it met the skin of his face. She had stared at his face for hours. Fascinated by everything, even by the slightly open pores on his nose. By the way the hairs grew on his top lip, the way his ears joined onto his head, even his spots. She had thought that meant she loved him, but looking at him now she wasn't sure.

How could he have done that? She shuddered—no—she was making it up. He pulled another tissue out.

'It's bleeding like mad,' he said and threw the old one in her bin.

'Why are you asking, then?' Stefanie walked over to the bin and turned it around with her foot, so the picture on the front (which was of some crap boy band she had liked in Year Seven) was facing the other way.

'Worried.' Mark shrugged.

'Worried?' Stefanie coughed. She was aware she sounded a bit too much like her mother. 'You're not worried about him. I bet you don't even know his name.' Stefanie wanted more than anything for him not to have done it. But then why was he here asking this stuff? What could she say?

Mark said nothing. He sat on her bed chewing his nails. Guilty, thought Stef. Maybe he wants me to lie about where he was. Maybe he wants me to cover up for him. Stefanie felt sweat coming. Prickling.

'Say you didn't do it.'

'Of course not.' He sounded tired now.

'Why are you here, then?'

'I was worried.'

'You said that.'

'About you as well,' Mark said. Stef didn't look round. 'I heard something—something about it. I was worried OK. OK?'

'Well, I'm all right.' She folded her arms. 'He's not though, couldn't have been. They had breathing stuff—tubes—and all sorts out of the ambulance.'

'Sometimes, right, things look a lot worse than they are.'

'You never saw him.' Stef stared at Mark. He stared back. He dabbed at his thumb.

'I took his picture.' She knew she shouldn't have said it but now she had maybe it could be a test. A sort of test.

'With the police there?'

'No. It was before.'

'Can I see?'

'I haven't done them yet.' Stefanie looked at him. 'I'll do them tomorrow at school.'

Mark breathed out slowly. 'You're all right then?'

'What does it look like?' Stefanie even smiled at him. She wanted him to say he didn't do it and to hug him up right now. She wanted him to kiss her, but he sat on the bed, nervous. Scared even.

'I'm off then.' He got up without warning. Maybe, Stef thought, me smiling at him is scaring him off. 'Catch you later.'

'What?' Stefanie felt like she'd missed something. 'When later?'

'Later. I'll phone.' He picked up his bag and headed for the door.

Stefanie watched him go from the kitchen window. He had his hands full of fishing stuff and his shoulders were stiff. But that was how he always walked. Maybe, Stef thought, there was someone waiting for him round the corner. Maybe he was just worried about her. But how did he know about what had happened? Why did he care?

As soon as he'd gone she phoned Becky. But that was a mistake. 'I'm grounded for a month.' Stefanie heard Becky sigh so loud she had to move the phone from her ear. 'And it's probably not a good idea for you to come round. You're not exactly Mum's favourite person right now.'

Stefanie knew what to expect. Becky's parents seemed to think their lovely daughter would never go off with a boy she didn't know, to a party she wasn't invited to.

'They think it's all me. Don't they?' It wasn't worth getting angry about. 'Anyway, I never phoned you about that.'

'What then?'

'Shahid. You know.'

'Yeah.'

'Well, this morning, just now, Mark comes round. Asking stuff.'

'What stuff?'

'About last night. Like did we see anything. Like did Shahid say anything.'

'Just now he came round? How did he know?'

'I don't know. I really don't. I didn't think.'

'So do you think he did it? Him and his mates? My Gavin and Mark? Never! Did he say how he knew?'

'I never asked. Didn't think till he'd gone. I know, I

know I'm stupid. Beck, you won't say anything, all right? Anything. I don't know. I mean, I didn't think he could. I thought I knew him. I really did.'

Stefanie felt her insides dissolving into soup. Why else would he have come round now? How else would he have known? Why did it have to be Amina's brother—someone she knew? Somehow it felt like she, Stefanie, had done it herself. As if she had kicked Shahid's nose half off his face.

The afternoon was hot and thick. The tar in the car park had gone soft in places and some of the little kids were hopping about in it. Making shapes. The sky was heavy with old car smoke and it hung between the ground and the sky like a veil. A chador—or is it hijab? Stef thought. It might drop and cover everyone. Suffocate everything. Stef remembered Mark and little cold bumps came on her arms. Maybe *he* would suffocate her. Maybe she wanted that. If she just wanted the feeling of closeness. The feeling of his skin up next to hers—if she wanted that—it would be so easy to just shut her eyes and let him smother her. It wouldn't matter if her model didn't work, if she gave up taking pictures. She could just be his girlfriend. It would be so easy just to do that, to let it happen. Shut my eyes, Stefanie thought, shut my eyes and think about him. Then I don't exist.

9

Stefanie hadn't seen Amina leave the flat even though she'd been watching. She didn't want to bump into her or have to talk to her but then maybe she'd be off school today anyway. Stefanie waited until five to nine then bolted down the steps and out of the estate.

'Missed the bus, love?' one of the builders called. 'Cheer up, it may never happen.'

Stefanie wished what remained of the tower block would collapse and bury them. Outside the newsagent's on the corner there was a board for the *East End Herald*— the local paper. She had passed it before she realized what it said. 'ASIAN YOUTH IN GANG STABBING.' She ran back and bought a copy.

Her picture. The one she had taken of Shahid, the one she had given to Amina, was on the cover of the *Herald*. Shahid in the white snowboarding T-shirt. Grinning in his boffin glasses. The headline went: YOUTH, 18, IN STABBING HORROR. Stabbing horror, read Stefanie. More like kicking horror. Stefanie's stomach turned over as she remembered the last time she'd seen him. Nothing like that. Same T-shirt though.

The words of the article were racing and swimming on the paper and although she read them twice it still didn't make any sense. Intensive care. Serious but stable, it said. No evidence of racist attack, it said. Gang warfare on our streets. What kind of evidence did they need? Stef wondered. What kind of gangs did people think these were?

She imagined Shahid wired up to bleeping machines like her mother had been as an extra in that show *Emergency Alert*. But Mum had got up and washed the bruises and the blood off. Shahid's was all real.

It was quiet at school too. There was a special assembly—like when Kerry Lock had jumped off her balcony two years ago. The headmistress stood on the stage talking about intolerance, violence, ignorance. Stefanie let the words wash over her. Amina was staring straight ahead. Everyone else was trying not to stare at her—not obviously anyway. Mrs Roberts was standing next to her, hand on her shoulder. Pressing her down, thought Stefanie.

Stef also wondered why Amina was in school. Shouldn't she be down the hospital standing round the bed? Or in a side room waiting for news, drinking tea and weeping. Stefanie's mum would keep her off school if she sneezed, she liked the company, and then Mum wouldn't have to entertain the Whitmore twins. Which in Mum's case, Stef thought, meant turning the video on. Stef had given up on being ill a long time ago. Maybe Amina didn't want all that hanging around by the bed. Maybe she wanted things to be normal too.

The headmistress hadn't finished. She was still banging on about Shahid. Stefanie started counting the ropes at the side of the hall, just the ones that had knots in them. Then she started staring at the girl sitting in front of her who had really nasty split ends. All white and ragged. She imagined them fusing together and going all shiny like in shampoo adverts.

Then from the stage she realized the Head was talking about something else. A break-in. In the school darkroom and the media centre where they keep the video stuff. Equipment damaged, the headmistress said. Stefanie looked at the side of the hall for Mr Bartlett. He nodded at her. It was true. She went to look at first break. Bartlett came with her and she helped him clean up. Everything was smashed. All the enlargers, the trays, lightboxes. Strips of negs left hung up to dry were all over the floor. Bottles of developer tipped everywhere. Stef really thought she'd cry.

'Everything always gets ruined, sir, always.'

'Come on, Stefanie, cheer up. It's only things. Just things, not people.' Stefanie thought that things did matter sometimes. At least as much as some people. People were everywhere all the time. Messing things up. 'It must have been kids. Someone's idea of a laugh.' He lifted an enlarger back onto its table.

'But they never took nothing, sir.' Stefanie thought whoever had done it must be that daft not to take anything. Just to smash it all up.

'They took the video stuff mostly. Easier to carry and sell on.'

'I suppose you wouldn't get much for this anyway.'

Stefanie picked up several plastic trays and stacked them neatly again. She noticed the contact prints she'd done last thing on Friday. The ones she'd taken as a favour for Becky's mum, of Janice trying to look grateful in her new jumper, were all trodden into the floor. The negatives were ruined. She swept the broken bits and glass off the floor. Every last bit.

'Well, Stefanie, you're very good at this cleaning.' Mr Bartlett was almost unpleasantly jolly.

'Yes, sir,' Stef said flatly. 'I get a lot of practice at home.'

In her blazer pocket she could feel the hard round film case she had brought in to develop. The one with Shahid on—after he'd been beaten up. She closed her hand round it to make sure it was safe. By the look of things the school darkroom would be shut until after the summer holidays. She'd have to take it to a shop.

Becky reckoned someone was after them. 'I bet, Stef! I bet they think we know who did it. I bet!' Becky sat in front of her school sponge cake. Prodding the jammy bit until it leaked red into the yellow custard. 'I bet that's what Mark was on about. Trying to find out how much you know.'

Stefanie looked round the canteen. The sun was hot through the big glass windows and the smells from the kitchen were thick and sickly.

'I reckon it was Mark or someone. Martin said it could've been anyone. But I reckon the same people who did Shahid, did the darkroom.' She scooped a big spoonful of yellow and red into her mouth. 'I'd be that careful if I were you.'

'This isn't the telly, Beck. And anyway there's nothing in those photos but Shahid. You know that. We never saw anyone else.' Stefanie sighed. She was getting bored with thinking about it. Bored with the same thoughts going round and round. It couldn't be Mark. She told herself that every ten minutes.

Amina was sitting at a table nearest the double doors with her mates, all in black, some pulling their scarves lower over their heads. There wasn't much eating going on. Stefanie pushed her bowl away from her.

71

'I'll have that.' Becky finished hers and started on Stefanie's.

There was a place in Whitechapel by the station. 'Your photos in one hour,' it said. Snappy Snappy Snaps, in yellow letters. Normally Stefanie avoided these places.

'35 mm, black and white, please.' She passed the little plastic box across the counter keeping her hand on it until the last minute.

'Ooh! Black and white,' said the man. He was wearing a yellow Snappy Snappy Snaps cap. It was digging into his temples and Stefanie could see red marks on his forehead when he took it off. 'Don't have much call for that, love. Reckon it'll be nearer to two hours.'

Stefanie let go of the film and wandered out into the street. The hospital where Shahid had been taken was directly across the road. It was a big old building squashed by the helipad that sat on the top.

The pavement on this side of the road was wide and sloping and covered in market stalls from Vallance Road to the new Sainbury's. Even though the pavement was wide it was crowded—packed with people—buggies, bikes, all moving against each other. The ground was sticky with dirt and Stefanie felt the sweat trickling down the centre of her back collecting up against the waistband of her school skirt. She wanted to go home and have a cool shower. Wash the dirt off—wash everything off. Wash all the horrible thoughts away from inside her head. She paused by the crossing and pressed the button. WAIT lit up feebly, but Stefanie didn't want to. So she stepped off the kerb and pushed forward across the road through the static traffic towards home.

Stefanie got the photos later that evening. She had thought

72

of getting Becky or Leona to go with her. What if the shop people had shown the pictures to the police or something? She wished she had thought of that earlier. Her hands were shaking when she opened the paper wallet and she flipped quickly through them. The glossy paper made each picture slippery like water and she had trouble stopping them slithering onto the floor. There were the close ups of hands she'd been doing for Bartlett. Mark walking past the old chimney on the canal. Becky eating an ice cream. Becky and Leona outside the cinema. Getting closer now. This was it: one pencil grey five by seven smudgy rectangle. It hadn't come out at all. She flipped past it. One other smudgy rectangle, exactly the same.

Maybe it hadn't happened at all. Couldn't have—she didn't have the picture. Maybe it was better this way. Because then if there really was someone after her, there'd be nothing for them to find.

Mark hadn't phoned. Stefanie was dying to phone him, but couldn't think what to say. She had dialled his number often enough. Waited until it was picked up—but then she put it down straight away, heart beating.

She had rehearsed what she would say in her head. One version went like this: 'Forget it. Never think about it, pretend it never happened. Let's go round the empty flats on Sandford Street.' Near enough. Another one went: 'Mark, I've got to know if you did it. What were you doing at my place so early? How did you know? Tell me, you have to tell me.' Mildly hysterical like someone on the telly. But she hadn't worked out exactly *why* he had to tell her.

Stefanie would have liked to talk to her mum the way teenagers do in Australian soaps. But the hot weather seemed to be making Mum worse and the music louder.

Because Becky was grounded Stefanie couldn't see her out of school either. She felt cut adrift. Sort of floating away from real life into a parallel world where she had no friends and everyone was weird and twitchy.

She tried doing the photographs but that felt strange too. As if they had been taken by someone else. She took them out every night and stared at them. But now she couldn't tell if they really were any good or not. Maybe it was all a waste of time. Maybe she should try and get her speeds up and do a secretarial course next year like Leona. Get a job that at least paid something—in a building society or an office in the city.

There were some journalists in the car park. They were there most days now. Trying to get Amina on the doorstep— or trying to get one of the neighbours to complain about gang warfare. There was a woman with shiny hair and a man with a camera. Stefanie would have liked to talk to them. If Becky was around they'd have seen all her pictures by now. Stefanie avoided them, stared at them— but that was it.

By Friday Mark still hadn't phoned. Shahid was critical but stable and Stefanie was desperate. Mark always phoned. Maybe he'd chucked her or perhaps he was afraid of her— hated her. Stefanie couldn't wait any more. She put on the dress that Mark had said she looked nice in and went straight round after school.

Mark was up in his room being Brazil beating Italy convincingly in the second leg of some international league he'd set up with the Nintendo. Stefanie sat on the bed and moved her legs so that the skirt of her dress showed more of her thigh. She caught her reflection in his wardrobe mirror and pulled her skirt down and drew her knees together quick. Italy scored and Mark looked grim.

'You're still one up,' Stefanie said, smiling. Whatever had happened Stefanie still wanted everything to be all right. When it comes down to it, she thought, I'm more like Mum than I know. Wanting everything easy. But easy only ever worked short term.

Mark said nothing and Brazil kicked off again. The noise of the computer generated crowd filled up the quiet for a bit and Stefanie was glad. She fiddled with her hair and tried to think of what to say.

'You haven't phoned all week.' Stefanie slid off the bed and sat beside him on the floor. Truth, she said inside—don't kiss him—find the truth. Better not to know, Mum said inside her head. Stefanie stared at him staring at the telly. Flicking his thumbs on the control pad. Did she love him? OK, maybe not love. Maybe sometimes something like love. She had nothing to measure her feelings against. She knew she should hate him if he'd been the one to do Shahid. Somewhere she hated him, but she wanted to touch him. She sighed. A long sigh and Brazil took a corner and missed.

'Mark?'

'Hmm?'

'Nothing.'

If he had done it what was she going to do? Go to the police? Tell Amina? Tell Becky? What would happen? She'd have to go to court in her green school blazer and Mark would go to prison. He could be done for underage sex too, and then everyone would know. Stefanie sighed again. The football finished and Mark flicked the telly off.

'I thought you weren't phoning me,' Stefanie said at last.

Mark shrugged. Stefanie felt the shrug like a wave of cold coming off him.

'Do you want to talk?' Cool, thought Stef, be cool.

'I'll talk.' He put a tape on and sat next to her on the floor, so that his leg touched hers. In her head Stefanie pulled away and shouted at him—admit the truth, tell me everything. But in real life she left her leg against his, pressing it closer.

'Shahid. That boy, last week. He lives downstairs from us.'

'Yeah?' Mark said it like he'd never known. But it had been all over the papers. 'Mate of yours, then?'

'No! 'Course not.' Inside a knot came hard in her stomach. I did know him. But she didn't say it out loud.

'Haven't seen you all week.' Mark still didn't look at her.

'You said you'd phone,' Stef said.

'I reckoned you would.'

Stefanie shrugged. It had turned out like Becky said it would. The two of them sitting, saying nothing. Becky would have shouted at him. 'You used me!' she'd have said. But Stefanie knew she had used Mark. For sex, for company, for something. People use people, that's what they're for. Use them for a photo. Use them to moan at. To walk you home. To tell you what to wear—how to do anything. Everyone uses. Stefanie felt sad. She shifted her leg away from his. She didn't want to come over as desperate.

Through the window on the far side of the canal, a small black bird—a moorhen, Stef thought—waddled out across the towpath. It was walking funny like its legs were tied together. It was peeping, wide open red beak, as if it thought someone could help it. Stefanie had seen birds by the canal before with fishing line caught round their legs and you couldn't get near them. They'd be screaming—as near screaming as birds can do anyway. Hobbling, and flailing their wings. So you'd try and get near and help them but they always crashed into the water, or if they could manage it flew away.

Stefanie sighed. This was getting boring. She shut her eyes and remembered Shahid.

'Tell me,' she said.

'Tell you what?'

'Everything. You know, all of it.'

'You'll wish I never had.'

Mark said it was Bishop Arnolds. Thought Shahid—or whatever his name was—was Shadwell. Well, he might've been. Paki anyway, innit. He was unlucky. Could have been any Paki. They were all dead scared at Bishop Arnold now—'cause it wasn't just any Paki, was it? It was some heavy gang stuff—not just schoolkids. They were shitting themselves, Mark said. He reckoned Stefanie should know 'cause she was Becky's mate. And hasn't Becky got a brother? And Stefanie said, of course she's got a brother and Mark goes, there you are.

'Martin?' Stefanie couldn't believe it. 'Are you saying it was Becky's Martin?'

'I never said that.'

'Martin and his lot?'

'You asked.' Mark flicked the telly on. Stefanie stood up. She couldn't speak.

'So I'll phone, then?' Mark said, not looking round.

Stefanie nodded. Stefanie knew he wouldn't though. She knew it had finished and she knew it was easier not to make a scene. Enough scenes. Her head was full of imagining Martin and his mates doing Shahid.

Stefanie went down to the canal to look for the moorhen but it had gone. She couldn't even hear it now. She stood on the towpath, looking up and down. She must have been standing there for half an hour waiting, watching the patterns on the water, but nothing happened. There was no point knowing something if you couldn't do anything about it.

10

The first weekend without Mark for months. Stefanie thought she'd go up that art shop in Brick Lane and buy card. Try and sort her pictures out. Heavy white mounting board with a totally subtle texture you could only see when the light hit it a certain way. It would be pricey, but she had some saved—and she knew where Mum put the child-minding money if she didn't have enough. Mum wouldn't mind if it was for school and this was sort of school. Kitchen table drawer under the torn-open electricity bill envelopes. The drawer wouldn't open all the way. Stefanie snaked her wrist through the gap and fished around among old papers, birthday cake candle holder things, and broken pens.

It was no good. She needed the drawer right open. She pulled her hand out and thumped the table hard to unjam it. Jiggled it—right left, right left—pulled hard. Then the whole drawer whomped onto the kitchen lino shedding papers on the way. Stefanie got down onto the floor and began scooping them up: old school reports, bills, postcards from Nan from Devon and the Lake District. A fat flat wallet full of photographs. Stefanie pulled it out and sifted through them.

Stefanie stared. She was conscious of her bottom jaw falling further away from her face. It was Mum—her mum—with ridiculous brown and red streaks, 'Lo-lights, darling', that dated it to the late seventies—before I was born, Stef thought—and entirely stupid spike-heeled grass-green sandals that did up in bows around her ankles. There was an ankle chain too—just visible if Stefanie screwed up her eyes a bit. Her mother's lips looked pink and shiny as they spat out bubblegum and the shape of her mouth formed a perfect and unnatural 'O'. Surprised. She was supposed to be looking surprised. Brainlessly surprised as she pulled open the shiny green bikini top. Maybe Mum was surprised that her nipples could be so pink.

The glossy paper and lurid colours made Stefanie's head swim and she could feel the lunchtime take-away curry rising up from her stomach.

How could her mother be so stupid. It hurt Stefanie to look. But she couldn't stop. Rear view. Front view. Close up. Smiling. Pouting. Legs apart. Eyes shut. Mouth open. Everything.

Suddenly Mum was there, next to her. Peering over her shoulder. 'Oh,' she said, flicking her ash out of the window. 'You found those.'

Stefanie said nothing, but looked hard into her mother's face. What was worse—what was even more annoying— was that she, Mum, was smirking, chewing down the corners of her mouth to stop the grin getting out.

'I only did it for the money, love.'

'I wasn't thinking it was art, Mum.'

Stefanie's face said 'How could you?' Stefanie couldn't

imagine Amina's perfect dead mother having anything to do with this. Stuff like this. She flipped another one out. Mum with her naked pinky bum in the air. It hurt to look. Or Becky's mother even, a decent mother, posing nude at her knitting machine. They were proper mothers.

'If we needed money why couldn't you get a sewing machine, or do Christmas crackers like everyone else?'

'Oh, Stef.' Mum laughed. 'Sometimes I wonder if you're a daughter of mine, I really do.'

Stefanie began to shake.

'I mean,' Mum went on, 'look at this one.' She waved it under Stef's nose. 'If you'd have said "Why are you wearing such naff sandals?" that'd be different. Come on, love! It was only a step or two away from all those cheesy walk-ons in halter necks and hotpants.'

Stefanie felt the tears coming. Why did she have such a useless mother, what had she done to deserve her? There had been a time when Stef was little when Mum had been reasonably normal, almost just like anyone else. Even if she had to get used to seeing her mum in the background of some nappy advert, or not noticing the difference between butter or margarine on the telly, she had still been a proper sort of mum. Still picked her up from school and sewn clothes labels in her uniforms, made Rice Crispy cakes for the school jumble sales sometimes, that sort of thing.

After Year Five or Six that had all gone out of the window. Mum had even forgotten to take her to the dentist for three years. Three entire years. What if she'd needed braces like that Deniece in Year Nine? Or if they'd gone black and fallen out? In the end she had only got it together when Stefanie had broken her tooth on a crusty bloomer at Nan's.

Mum stubbed the cigarette out on the wall outside the window and flung the end out into the car park.

'Come off it, love, it's not that bad. I think my bum's sort of all right in this one.'

'You would.' Stefanie felt even angrier. How did she know how bad anything was, she didn't even live in the real world.

'I tell you what though, I'd do it again if I still looked that good. It's the stretch marks see.' She lifted up her T-shirt and Stefanie winced. 'Your Nan said olive oil. Rub it in every day, and I did try that, went around smelling like salad dressing for months! But you were such a big baby! I had to have stitches and everything. Didn't sit down for a week, and I was so fat!' Mum smiled, remembering. 'You know, I thought no one would ever want to look at me again.'

'No one would want to look at you, you're old.'

'Thirty-nine, lovey, don't rub it in.'

Stefanie looked her mother up and down. Her hair was shiny but unbrushed, she hadn't done her make-up yet either and her eyes seemed small. The skin round her eyes was thin and wrinkly, even though Mum slapped on enough eye rejuvenating creme with active liposomes to unwrinkle rhino skin.

'They're just pictures, lovey, just photos. I mean.' Mum moved over to Stefanie and rubbed her on the back. Stefanie flinched. 'It's not real, it's not something I did more than once or twice.'

'You've probably been in loads of slaggy porn movies. Loads, I bet, wouldn't put it past you!' The word that popped into Stefanie's mind was slut, but she couldn't bear to say it out loud to her mother. Mum was smirking again. Stefanie couldn't bear how little her mother seemed to feel about real things, not just stupid songs.

'How could you do this?' Stefanie said it as a whisper.

Mum sat down. 'Ah, Steffi love. That's not me.'

'Don't lie, I hate your lies.'

'It was me—once—for a few seconds. But it's not me forever. The camera just holds a bit of life and flattens it. Says: this is real, and bugger the rest, forget what happens round it, like what you look like when you've just got up, or how you're going to get the money for the skating lessons, or what you're making for tea. It's not interested. It just wants you for a few seconds and over. Done with, trashed. That's not your precious truth or reality any more than this.' She waved her hands around the flat. 'Mine goes on in here, here,' she pointed at her head. 'This doesn't, these pictures don't matter, it's just a laugh. I mean if I can laugh at them . . . '

'I can't.'

'Maybe one day, lovey, when you're older.'

Stefanie felt herself shaking. 'Don't give me that wise stuff, that clever stuff, that it'll all be better when I'm older stuff.'

Mum made a strange gurgling noise that Stefanie knew was a stifled laugh. She stared hard at her mother, hoping she could feel exactly how angry she was. She wanted daggers to be shooting out of her eyes, she wanted a stake through Mum's heart, a machine gun to cut her down. She imagined pushing Mum hard over the balcony wall, watching her land in the car park in slow motion, bouncing off the car roofs, slamming into the concrete, just like the movies.

Then she remembered that Mum was much better at being hysterical than she could ever be. Try cool, she thought. Mum could never take cool. She breathed in deep.

'I hate you.' Stefanie said it calmly. Her mother's face fell. Good.

'Stefanie?' Mum's voice was wobbly. Good.

Stefanie kept on staring. 'I hate you. No wonder Dad never wanted to live with you.' The magic bullet.

Stefanie could see the tears welling up in the bottom of Mum's eyes. Bull's-eye.

'Stef, love. I really didn't think you'd mind. Not now, now you're almost grown up, love. Stef?' Mum had crumpled entirely.

Stefanie put the photos down and walked out of the flat. She was going to slam the door and make the block shake, but then she remembered the journalists in the car park and closed it quietly. She leant over the landing wall and began counting, slowly for seconds. She had got to six before the music started up. The two reporters looked up at her; Stefanie just smiled. Stefanie recognized the intro. R-E-S-P-E-C-T. How could Mum have the nerve to play that *now*. How did she expect anyone to respect her? Stefanie wiped the wet out of her eye and sniffed.

First off Stefanie thought it was a rubbish bag. A lumpy black sack propped up against the landing wall. But it was Amina dressed in a black hooded winter coat, sitting on a nylon bag. Her legs were tucked up so that the points of her shoes stuck out from under the front of her coat.

'Hi.' Stefanie sat down next to her. 'What's up?' She bit her tongue. Of course she knew—everyone did. 'Sorry.'

'That's all anyone ever says these days. I mean, it's not as if it is your fault.'

'No. Sorry.' They sat there not saying anything. Amina making the toes of her black shiny shoes clack together. Stefanie imagined telling Amina everything. Imagined Shahid making a total recovery and everyone shaking her hand and thanking her and saying what a wonderful girl she was. But it wouldn't be like that at all. They'd thank her all right—but Becky might never speak to her again.

Don't say anything, she thought. Then maybe Amina would go away. She didn't.

'I heard you in there, with your mum,' Amina said, still clacking her toes. Stefanie sighed. She didn't want to talk about that with anyone. Best change the subject.

'What are you doing here? Don't tell me you had a row with your dad.'

'Sort of. He doesn't want me here.'

'What?' Stefanie didn't believe it. 'What do you mean?'

'No, no. He wants me to stay at my auntie's, in Forest Gate. Says it's not good here on my own. Stuff comes through the door.'

'What stuff?'

'Dog mess.' Amina looked embarrassed.

'Dog shit. You're kidding!' Stefanie knew it happened in other places—on other estates—but not here.

'I don't care about that stuff. It's only those Parris kids anyway. They don't scare me.' Amina screwed up a chewing gum wrapper in her hand and let it fall off the balcony. Stefanie had her mouth open. Darryl Parris— she'd snogged him in Primary school. Maybe she only ever kissed racists.

'I just don't want to go. I want to be here with him and Shahid. I want to be here if anything happens. I mean, if it was your brother, or whatever, you'd want to be there. Not miles away on the other side of town. I mean—what if he dies? What if he dies and I never saw him?'

Amina stared up at the yellow sky. Stefanie saw the water welling up in her eyes and looked away. Change the subject again, something happy.

'Do you want to see my photos, of the flats?' Stef hadn't meant to say that at all. And now it was out she hoped Amina hadn't heard her. But she had. She nodded and smiled.

'Yeah.' Amina tried not to sniff and wiped her eyes with the back of her sleeve. 'Yeah. OK, I'd love that.'

The music was so loud Stefanie was sure Mum wouldn't hear them. The living room door was closed and the two girls crept past into Stefanie's room.

'Why does she do it?' Amina asked. 'Play that music so loud, I mean?'

Stefanie thought. 'I dunno. I suppose it stops her thinking. That's what she said once.'

'Thinking about what?'

'Life. I suppose: getting old, not getting a part working in the launderette with Pauline in *EastEnders*.' Stefanie smiled. 'I just wish she'd get some new tunes. She does my head in. Anyway, forget her. Get up on the bed and I'll get these pictures out.'

Stefanie took the photos out carefully, unwrapping each one from its tissue paper sleeve, and laid them out in order on the floor. 'See?' Stefanie felt suddenly nervous. 'See. It's like a record. It's like this block—only a block of people, not flats.'

Amina looked. Peering over the edge of the bed at the sea of pictures. Stefanie's heart was going worse than with Mark. She looked from Amina's face to the pictures and back again. Amina was concentrating at least, Stef thought. But then maybe that was because she was a boffin and always looked like that when she was thinking. Maybe she was thinking it was all crap.

'What do you think?' Stefanie couldn't wait.

Amina pushed her plait back behind her shoulders. 'It's lovely. Honest. I never imagined . . . ' Stefanie felt herself reddening. ' . . . I always wondered what you were up to. Seeing you with that camera. I thought: it's just going to be us all in the building, all looking, just looking ordinary. But all together, like this. It's like history.'

'Yeah, that's what I wanted. Like a record. I've got to mount them, though. Properly, neatly.'

Amina nodded, then she stopped. 'What about what's-her-name? Cat woman downstairs?'

'I know. She wouldn't let me.'

'Does that woman smell or what!' Amina giggled.

Suddenly the music stopped. Right in the middle of Marvin Gaye.

'Shhh!' Both girls froze. Then Stefanie heard the front door slam. 'God I hate her!' Stefanie sat down on her desk.

'Don't say that!' Amina was genuinely shocked. 'You can't say that!'

'You don't know her.'

'She's your mum—you should be glad you've still got one.'

Stefanie was quiet. She didn't think her mum was worth talking about. 'Were you close? You and him? Your brother?'

'He's not dead yet, you know.'

'Sorry, I didn't mean it like that. I meant . . . you know . . . did you . . . do you talk to him and that?'

'We lived in the same flat. Oh, I don't know. Sometimes I felt like he thought he should be the brainy one, and not just be hanging around the streets. It would be much easier then. He said he was getting too old, said horrible things about . . . ' Amina stopped, looked vague. 'About people . . . some people. Pointless stuff. But he'd only just got involved with the mosque. The young Moslems. He was a lot happier. But then he'd row with Dad. About me, about lots of things.' Amina sighed. 'Like, like suddenly he was the dad. I did think it was getting better though. He was eighteen last month. He just started signing on.'

Stefanie nodded. She'd never really felt scared of him,

like she felt about some of the boys he went with. 'He seemed all right to me.'

'I just wish all this would stop. I just wish the world would stop and I could think about something else. I just want Dad and Shahid to come walking right back up the steps to the flat. Anything—just normal—all normal.' Amina's eyes had gone watery again. Stefanie started putting the pictures away. 'I mean. Why was it us? I know he was bad sometimes, but he was never really bad. Like nicking stuff. Like bashing old ladies, was it? Was it?'

'No.' Stefanie sat next to her on the bed and rubbed Amina's back, the way her mum used to. Amina started sobbing. 'No,' Stef said again.

'I wish it was me. I wish it was me in hospital.'

'Come on. I'll make you a cup of tea. That's what I do for Mum.' Stefanie felt as if she needed to be doing something—anything—just moving around would be easier.

'I want to see him. I want to go and see him.'

Stefanie couldn't believe they hadn't let her. Amina explained her dad thought it would be too upsetting. Stefanie made the tea and Amina sat down at the kitchen table.

'Why don't you just go? It's not far. Just up Whitechapel.'

'I couldn't.' Amina shook her head.

'I'd come with you. Wait outside—whatever.'

'Would you? We'd never get in.'

'Why not?' Stef asked.

'Dad's there. All my uncles and that.' Amina stirred her tea. Stefanie thought she was going to start up crying again.

'There must be something you can do.'

'Yeah, get the tube to Forest Gate and pretend nothing's happening.'

'Pretend,' Stefanie said. 'You ought to talk to my mum about that. She's great at it. She can pretend whatever she likes. Whatever she wants.'

'She's lucky then.'

'I'm not. She doesn't pretend for me.'

'Look at us! Old women, drinking tea and moaning.' Amina smiled.

'See.' Stefanie pointed with her teaspoon. 'That's not really smiling, I can tell. That's changing the subject 'cause it's too difficult.'

'Yeah, well maybe sometimes it is too difficult. OK? Maybe your mum knows what she's doing.'

Stefanie nodded. She still couldn't say out loud her mum was right. 'You don't know my mum.' She thought of the photographs of Mum, shiny and stupid, and made a gulping noise. That wasn't the mother she wanted. Then she looked at Amina and felt guilty for feeling so sorry for herself.

'What do you want to do? Really. Not pretend.'

'I want to be there, to be with Shahid. I don't want to go to my auntie's.' Amina sighed. 'I just wish I was somewhere else.'

'Honest?'

Amina nodded. Maybe there was something Stefanie could do for her after all. Outside, through the window, Stefanie watched the swifts diving in the sky.

11

Although it was getting late there was a crowd outside the front of the hospital. Two crowds really, one on either side of the war memorial. On the right was the mosque lot. Stefanie was amazed. She didn't realize there would be so many people outside the hospital. She hadn't thought of that at all.

'OK, we'll have to do the hospital tomorrow,' Stefanie said.

'I told you it was impossible.'

'No way! Look, Amina, we'll get in there tomorrow, I promise. Trust me.' Stefanie walked faster past the hospital, Amina pulled her hood up and followed. Even though they were on the other side of the main road.

'They're from the Y.M.O. Shahid's mates. See? There's no way I can get in there.'

Stefanie looked anyway. She thought she recognized some of them—but it was hard to tell. A lot of them had white skullcaps and one had a megaphone. He was shouting stuff, but you couldn't hear it above the traffic noise.

The other lot looked scruffy in the way that some of the younger teachers did at school: DMs, funny hair. They had their own megaphone and lots of placards saying 'Stop Racist Violence NOW!' There were police too—a couple on horses and a van parked up on the pavement.

'I wonder where he is?' Stefanie could see hundreds of windows and that was just the front of the building.

'Someone might see me.' Amina pulled her hood down lower and walked faster. Someone might see me, Stefanie thought. See me out with Amina. Then she felt angry with herself for thinking that and smiled hard at Amina and led her up a side street.

'So where are we going now?' Amina asked.

Stefanie smiled. 'My surprise. You said you wanted to be somewhere else.'

Behind Whitechapel the streets were a mix of narrow alleys and old buildings almost falling down and not so new flats also nearly falling down. Just like hers, Stef thought. The bollards were all cannons, Becky had told her, from some ancient war, stuck into the Victorian cement to stop the horses driving on the pavement. Some of the houses had been done up—with painted shutters and ornate porches—but mostly it was falling down.

Stefanie thought the city farm was the best place to go. Not too far away, no people, and she knew how to get in. It'd be fun. Not really running away. More like camping out. A joke—a buzz. She was helping Amina out and no one would know.

The street was empty. There was one small block of flats, then the massive railway bridge that carried the main line out of Liverpool Street. The little wooden fenced fields were empty too. The city farm had massive double gates. Painted with a happy hippy mural of children and animals, only just visible in the dark. Amina pushed against them and they moved swinging slightly inwards.

'That's not the way,' Stefanie whispered, even though there was no one around. 'We have to get around the back.'

There were some allotments and Stefanie showed Amina how you could squeeze in through a gap in the wire fence. Then all they had to do was climb up onto the roof of the farm's dairy and jump down into the yard. Stefanie had been with Becky and Gavin and some others one night last summer. They'd got in and mucked around. They'd had some drinks and some smokes. It had been fun letting the chickens out and chasing them. Gavin had found a pot of white paint and was about to paint 'Arsenal' on the donkey's back until the girls persuaded him that was cruel. They rounded up all the chickens after and put them back. Well, as many as they could. No harm done really.

Stefanie and Amina got onto the dairy roof. It was corrugated iron and more slippery than Stef had remembered. But what was worse was that it was dark—pitch black by London standards. So far from the street lights that jumping into the yard looked like jumping down into a black hole.

'You're mad, Stefanie! Mad! We'll break our legs!'

'No, listen. I've done it before, OK? It's OK. I'll go first. I'll show you, honest.'

Inside Stefanie was thinking it would be better to go home now, OK, so Mum wouldn't get really worried, but Amina's dad . . .

Stefanie shut her eyes and jumped.

'See, see! I said didn't I!' She put her bag down and held her arms out for Amina. 'Jump! I'm here!'

'I don't believe I'm doing this.' Amina jumped and

both girls stood giggling in the yard not quite holding each other.

'I think I did my ankle.' Amina was still laughing.

'Rubbish! You're all right. Come on, I'll show you where we're sleeping.'

The animal sheds were all padlocked but Stef remembered that there was a hayloft, where they kept bales of straw and that above the stable. It would be perfect. It was even darker up there and the noise of the big horse breathing in the stall below them was scary and soothing at the same time.

'We're all right.' Stefanie smiled at Amina before she realized she couldn't see her anyway. Maybe she could hear the smile. Amina made a nervous, almost laughing, sound.

'It's like camping,' Stefanie said.

'Have you been then?'

'No.'

'Nor me neither.'

Outside a train went over the railway viaduct and it shuddered and creaked. It was a huge long slow night time train. Containers, Stefanie thought, heading for the Essex coast. The noise went on for ever and when it did stop Stefanie had forgotten what they'd been talking about. She shifted on the bales of straw, trying to get comfortable, but it was so prickly. There was a gap where her neck came out of her jacket and Stefanie could picture the hard yellow stalks digging into her skin. There could be insects too—spiders and beetles with black shiny backs waving their legs and other things in the air. Stefanie sat up. Through the gap in the wooden wall she could see out over the farmyard and just make out the sheep moving and rustling in the barn.

'You OK?' Amina sat up too.

'Itchy. It's this straw.' Another train passed. The horse

sighed and shook in its sleep. 'I never knew they slept standing up,' Stef said. 'I mean, I never believed it. Mum told me once but I never really believed her. Funny innit, standing up.'

'I read that somewhere.'

'Yeah, well, you're a boffin, we all know that.'

'OK. OK.'

'Sorry. I didn't mean it like . . . sorry.'

'I don't mind. It's just boring. I can't help being clever.'

'I wouldn't know. It must make it easier though sometimes. You know, college and that. You can just walk it. You could go anywhere.'

Stef heard her shrug. 'Dunno. See . . . Shahid . . . ' Amina made a little swallowing noise. 'Shahid thinks it's a waste of time.'

'Never! He's not like that.'

'Don't you believe it. He's worse than Dad. He says he knows girls who go to college. He says he knows what they're like.'

'You're kidding me. Really? Your brother?'

'Yup.' Amina nodded.

'But he's so . . . '

'So what? So trendy? See him in his trainers? Oh yeah! See him with his "brothers", hanging out. I know what you're thinking. But he is worse than Dad. Dad, my dad, is cool. He used to be all for it—college and that. The teachers—especially Haworth in Chemistry—giving him earfuls about his brilliant daughter. Then he comes home and he's getting it from Shahid. Every day little things. You know, building it up. Little things.'

'Like what?' Stefanie was lost.

'I reckon he's just jealous. Telling some story to Dad about so and so's cousin going to university and never getting married. Or someone's sister going to college and meeting boys. English boys—any boys—and going to dances. You know.'

'Is this for real, what you're saying?'

'Yup.'

'So you're not going.' Stefanie couldn't believe it.

'Don't look like it.' Amina was quiet. 'I don't hate him like that though, you know. He's only doing his best.'

'If he was my brother . . . '

'OK. End of subject, all right. I don't want to talk about it.'

'Sorry.' Stefanie shifted in the straw. 'So what'll you do then? You know?'

'What am I, Mystic Meg?'

'I dunno. I thought it was easy for you to do what you want. Live on your own.'

'I don't want to be on my own.'

'No, I mean away from your family. Don't you? That's my idea of heaven.'

'I don't mind all that husband and babies stuff. Honest! I'd love kids, me.'

'You can't be that much of a boffin then.'

'Shut it, you. I fancy a big wedding—big party—the works. Dancing in the evening, everyone happy. Great dress. I'd have this really great dress.'

'That's what you want? Really?'

'Yup.'

'I don't believe it.' Stefanie thought that Mum had knocked all those ideas on the head for her. She wouldn't do it like that. She would have a job—and not just part-time in some poxy shop either.

Another train rumbled back the other way into Liverpool Street. Becky had said once those trains carried nuclear waste. Stefanie imagined one careering off the viaduct into the farmyard. Hanging down from the track like a paper chain and bursting into flames. Leaking wisps of green smoke or doing whatever nuclear waste did.

'Will your dad choose? You know, choose?'

'Choose what?'

'You know . . . your husband?'

Amina sighed. An angry sigh. 'That's all you lot are ever interested in, ever. It's weird to you lot that our parents actually take an interest in our husbands and that. But you lot would just jump into bed with anyone. Even if you didn't know his family or hadn't even met his parents. Even if you never knew his name, I bet. That—if you're asking me—is about a hundred times—no, a million times—weirder. Doing that—that!—with someone you don't really know.' Stefanie rustled uneasily. 'Doing that with someone you've been out with a couple of times. Or you just met at a party. He could end up being some kind of lunatic. I mean, if you just thought, just thought for ten—no—five minutes only. Just thought about marriage. About life. About how well your parents actually know you. About life . . . '

'Look, I'm sorry I asked, OK? It was just a question. It was just something. Something I couldn't imagine. That's all.'

'Well try. OK? It works, doesn't it?'

'I'm sorry. All right. I'm sorry. It's just I couldn't trust my mum to choose my knickers for me.'

Outside a car stopped and the geese started honking.

'Shhh!' Stefanie and Amina lay totally still. Then the horse started scraping its shod hooves through the straw against the concrete floor. The geese stopped. It was quiet again.

'Have you got a boyfriend then?' Amina asked.

'I don't think so.' How could she admit to Mark now? After what Amina had said.

'Come on! Either you have or you haven't.'

Stefanie shrugged. She hoped Amina heard it.

'I met a boy once, I did. On a train.'

'See. Your brother's right, you do need watching.'

'No. Listen, I was on the way to a wedding with Dad. Up north it was. He was a student—twenty I think—with a moustache and everything. Made me look like a total dimbo.'

'Who was he then, Einstein? No, no, his kid brother.'

'No! He was going to be an astronaut.'

'He was having you on.' Stefanie laughed.

'No. Honest. He showed me the letter. European Space Agency.'

'Never heard of it.'

'It's true! Really, he wasn't going in a rocket, not yet. Just weightlessness training. Doing experiments and that in the upper atmosphere.'

'Oh yeah. Really convincing.'

'No I'm serious. He was!'

'What, the first Bengali in space?' Stefanie laughed. 'He had you taped, didn't he.'

'It's all true. You'll read about him one day, I bet. And you'll be taking his picture. I bet.'

'I bet you'll see him walking down the Commercial Road on his way to work in his uncle's restaurant. Just like everyone else.'

'I don't care if you don't believe me. That's what I want. Someone like that. Not like my brother's friends who won't go to school 'cause they never liked the colour of the jacket. Not like that.'

'You want your astronaut? Aaah.'

'Me and him, weightless, I'd love that.'

'You'd never get all your hair in the helmet.'

'I'd cut it.' Amina smiled in the dark.

12

Stefanie couldn't remember falling asleep but the noise of the geese and a passing train made her wake up instantly. The light was falling into the loft through the wooden slatted walls, lighting up dust like sparkles. Amina was snorting—and beyond that noise and the chickens and the geese and everything else she could hear the market starting up.

This was just so stupid, Stefanie thought. Stupid as anything she had ever done. They would have to go back and everything—whatever Amina had with her dad and whatever was left of Stefanie's family life with her mother—would be harder to fix. Somehow going home looked more difficult than running away. Her stomach rumbled and Stefanie thought that thinking about food was probably easier to work out than thinking about life. Stef imagined Mum and in her head put on 'Say A Little Prayer' top volume. Don't think about life, she thought. Think about food.

She looked through a crack in the wall. Anytime, it could be anytime—she'd left her watch at home. The people would come and open up the farm and shop. They had to get out.

'Amina.' Stefanie shook her. 'Amina, come on.'

Amina stretched out in the straw and opened her eyes—blinking in the light. Stefanie was already unrolling the coat she had slept on and brushing the bits of straw off her top. Her whole body felt stiff and creaky and she wondered how long the two of them could last out. Amina had lost her glasses in the straw and it took a good five minutes scrabbling around. The horse heard them and began scraping the ground. Stefanie looked down at it. In the daylight it looked huge and dangerous. Amina must have thought so too.

'Is that the only way out? Past that?'

The steps to the yard went down the side of the stable. If it had wanted to the horse could stretch its neck out and bite them.

'Don't be daft. What's it going to do? Breathe on us?'

'It's got teeth. It could bite.' Amina was not happy.

'It didn't bite us last night. Anyway, they're vegetarian,' Stefanie said. 'Aren't they?'

The horse ignored them and they made it back over the wall and into the allotments.

'Where are we going now?' asked Amina.

Stefanie wished she'd thought this whole thing out more. 'I dunno. The market. Get some breakfast. I'm starved.'

There were some stairs over the viaduct. They smelt of piss and were narrow and scary even in the daylight. But Stefanie insisted it was the quickest way. Over the other side and down into the street it was another world. Cheshire Street was full and it was still not seven o'clock. Stalls of clothes and junk, and a tape stall blaring out Irish ballads.

'I've never been here so early,' Amina said.

Stefanie's mum had had a stall here once years ago with one of her mates selling second-hand clothes. Good stuff though, Stefanie said. So she'd seen it all before. It was mostly junk. 'Antiques, love,' the stallholders said. Junk and old clothes and trays of jewellery. Amina wanted to look.

There was one tray full of name brooches. 'Victorian, they are, darling.' Agnes and Georgina and Emma, circled by tiny metal flowers. Amina tried on some hats and Stefanie forgot the empty feeling in her tummy and joined in.

'Urrgh, look at this!' It was a dead fox. Flattened and made into a scarf, its jaws opened and acted as a clasp.

'That is sick,' Stefanie winced. 'I mean, sick.'

There was a plastic baby bath full of old tools: hammers and spanners; and a furry rocking horse with one metal rocker.

Stefanie wandered over to the tape stall. Maybe she could interest her mother in something other than sixties Motown. Maybe she could shift her out of her timewarp. It was stupid really, 'cause Mum was only just born when all that music was made. In fact Mum had told her she'd been a punk once. Stefanie knew it was true because she'd seen the pictures. All purple hair and trousers with the legs tied together so you could only take small steps.

The bagel shop was packed and the queue stretched out of the shop and onto the pavement. It smelt like heaven: warm bread, coffee, and doughnuts. Stef and Amina joined the end of the queue behind some girls in tiny satin skirts who looked like they'd been up all night. One had blue mascara that had stuck clumps of eyelash together in globs. Another had just the waxy trace of lipstick colour left in the grooves of her lips. In front of them was a man with a tattoo—you could see a panther's claws reaching out from under the sleeve of his T-shirt.

Stefanie and Amina bought cream cheese bagels and two doughnuts each and ate until they felt sick and their fingers were coated with sugar. Amina was grinning.

'I don't think I was ever this hungry.'

Stefanie thought that for a boffin she was all right.

'What are we going to do now then?' Amina was almost like one of the Whitmore twins sometimes. Stefanie would have said go home but Amina was obviously having a good time. It was like the stuff with Shahid hadn't happened.

'Walk around?' Stefanie shrugged.

They walked out of the lane and over to the old fruit market, where there were loads more stalls and fairground rides. They went on a swing boat and the dodgems and drank frothy hot chocolate with big squirts of cream in. Amina was sure she saw Mr Helmsly their Maths teacher outside the organic butcher's, so they ran out of the covered market and didn't stop until they'd reached the huge white church on the other side of the road.

'He never saw us. He never.' Stefanie was still panting. The church steps were white too and there were loads of them up from the pavement. A party of Japanese tourists all wearing blue baseball caps were standing halfway up listening to a woman with a rolled up umbrella and a big badge that read 'Historic London: Guide' in blue letters.

'One of Hawksmoor's churches that are scattered throughout the East End,' she said. 'Eighteenth century,' she went on.

Stefanie pulled Amina along the steps and into a crowd of 'Jack the Ripper's London' tourists. 'Try and look interested,' Stefanie said. Amina smiled a daft 'I am interested' smile and Stefanie rolled her eyes. 'Stupid!'

The Jack the Rippers were led by a women in a Victorian low-cut frock. She had a crochet shawl and badly pinned up long red hair. Stefanie felt herself going choky looking at her.

'Stef, Stefanie? Are you OK?' Amina looked concerned. Stefanie wiped the wet away from her eyes. The woman looked like Mum when she had been Nancy in *Oliver Twist* at the Bow Assembly Halls. It was a green dress. The same colour as Mum's eyes. All shiny and worn at the same time. Mum loved that dress, how she looked in that dress. She said she was too old to play Nancy now. Stefanie sniffed. She could just remember going backstage with Nan. Seeing Mum. She was smiling so wide—so happy. Smelling the smell of the make-up and the sweat and the dressing-up theatre clothes. Stefanie wished Mum was old enough to be Mum.

'Yeah, 'course.' Stefanie wiped her eyes quickly. She was being stupid. Amina's brother in hospital and all I'm doing is going weepy for my loopy mother.

The Rippers and the Japanese moved off and Stefanie and Amina were on their own. Standing on the steps above the sea of people and traffic on Commercial Street.

'Let's go in.' Amina was pulling at her. 'Let's go in the church, right?'

Stefanie was just about to follow Amina into the black hole that looked like the doorway when she spotted something square and red and yellow halfway up the steps. She ran down, picked it up and stuffed it into her pocket. It was one of those disposable cameras.

'Hang on, Amina.' Stefanie ran after her into the dark of the church.

Amina was sitting down in the dark. She patted the seat next to her.

'Sit here.' Amina was quiet. Head bowed.

'What are you doing?'

'Praying, innit.'

Stefanie leant back on the bench. It was huge and cool and old and quiet. She liked that. But praying?

'I thought you were Muslim.'

'It's one God, though. Same God. You can pray anywhere you like, I reckon.'

'Does it fix anything, though?' Churches made her cold.

Amina shrugged, head down. 'I'm praying for Shahid.'

Stefanie got up and walked around. She'd never been one for old things and this was really old.

'Oh my God, I'm walking on dead people!' Stefanie froze. The floor was all stone flags, all gravestones of people buried in the church. She made little inching steps round the edge of every separate stone back to Amina.

'We're going. Now!'

Amina smiled. 'You scared of dead people?'

Stefanie ran out into the light and down the steps. When Amina came out into the sun, blinking, Stef took her picture with the funny disposable camera.

'What are we doing?' Amina said. Stefanie had bought lollies, the big chocolate ones with ice cream inside. 'I don't know why I'm here, you know, with you. I'm going to get killed.'

Stefanie almost said something out loud about guilt—about feeling responsible, and about nothing mattering. But she just smiled instead and they walked back along Fashion Street to the Lane.

Brick Lane was crammed with people, loads of people. So many people it took ten minutes just to cross over to the far side. Stefanie was halfway across when she realized she was the only white person she could see. She felt lost in this brown soup of people. All talking a language she didn't understand, all together, and she was apart.

'Amina!' Stefanie wanted to wriggle out of the crush and back down Fashion Street to the covered market and the safety of other white people. 'Amina!' She couldn't see her anywhere. This is what it must be like for her all the time, Stef thought. All the time with the other. With a sort of person who looked different and dressed different. And you go up west and they're all like that. All white and talking funny and you don't belong. Stefanie looked round again. Most people were smiling. Lots held posters of Shahid. Posters of her photo blown up. It was for Shahid. All these people were here for Shahid. Amina burst though the brown towards her.

'It's Shahid's march!' She was grinning. Breathless.

'I can see that, can't I.'

'They're going to the hospital. I heard. To protest— you know. All these people!'

'Aren't you scared someone'll see you?'

'I don't know if I care any more.' She was dancing round. A bit too mad, Stef thought.

'You're on some sugar rush, you.'

Amina stopped twirling. 'The damage is done.'

They were carried down Brick Lane with the marchers. Stefanie had no idea what they were saying. The shouts indistinct and strange like the shouts of a football crowd on the telly. Stefanie took out the cardboard camera and pointed it at two tiny girls in red spangly dresses with shiny black hair pulled into identical tufts on their heads. They had fat brown arms and hands and fingernails with old chipped red varnish.

'I can't believe this is all for Shahid!' Amina started dancing again in the middle of the road, making a space for herself in the march. Stefanie had relaxed. It wasn't like carnival—not that relaxed—but everyone was together, shouting together, walking in step down the lane towards the hospital.

Amina was really enjoying herself. She had taken off the black hooded coat and tied it up around her middle. She was swirling and stamping in time with some drumming. Stefanie felt a little worried. Amina seemed just a little bit crazy, a little bit out there. Stefanie took her picture: grinning, plait flying, coat spinning out.

Then someone saw them. Mrs Uddin from the office at school and Amina deflated instantly like a balloon.

'Stefanie! Stefanie Clark!' Mrs Uddin was smiling. 'I didn't expect to see you here! And with Amina.'

Stefanie couldn't think what to say. Mrs Uddin was grinning so wide Stef thought her face would split. Thought her shiny brown skin might just zip apart.

'I'm taking pictures.' She held the camera up. 'See?'

And she snapped Mrs Uddin waving her placard. The photo of Shahid was bigger than Mrs Uddin's head and hovered just above her like a freaky cloud. The two-headed woman, Stef thought.

'See you, girls.' Mrs Uddin hugged Amina too hard. 'Tell your father we are with him.' Amina nodded. 'Your poor, poor father.'

Mrs Uddin vanished into the crowd and Amina breathed again. 'Stupid woman. It's not Dad, is it?'

'I suppose she's thinking if it was her son.'

'I know that!' Amina was furious. 'I know that! But it's not just Dad, is it? It's Dad and me and Shahid.'

'Listen, Amina, we'll go in the back of the hospital. Round the back. We can get in, I'm sure.' Stefanie paused. 'If that's what you want.'

Amina suddenly stopped. She was out of breath: too hot, sweaty faced. 'It's what I want.' She looked at Stefanie. Her face was flushed and her eyes were watery and far away. Stefanie didn't have a brother, she couldn't imagine what it was like. People hate their brothers. Becky did. Loves him—hates him. Sometimes. Stefanie thought Amina was lost. Up and down and off the rails. Like Mum.

The marchers slowed down outside the army surplus on the corner. Stef knew why. Here, every Sunday, about five or six men and sometimes women stood selling *White Nation*, and handing out leaflets which explained that the Holocaust had never happened, or why black people have smaller brains. One time Stef had been down with Becky and she had stared at them, really hard. Becky said they all looked the same those people: small mouths, dead eyes. Stefanie had nodded. But what she really thought was that they looked just like everyone else. Just like the man who came round from the council to do the ants or the weedy games teacher at school.

There was a line of policemen in front of the shop now. Sweating in their uniforms. Looking soft like melting ice creams. Stefanie took their picture. She felt a bit sorry for them being shouted and spat at. They had spots and flaky skin—just like real people. But then who were they supposed to be protecting? Stefanie looked at Amina, shouting and yelling. Not like Amina at school, sitting over a book and chewing her hair. She didn't need protecting now, but it was too late for Shahid.

Stefanie stayed close to Amina until they were almost at the hospital.

'Let's go,' Stef said, and they slipped out of the crowd and round to the back of the building. The entrance was smaller and the crowd and the marchers seemed miles away.

'Are you waiting for the dental clinic?' The receptionist didn't look up from her computer. Stefanie held on to Amina's coat, as if she was scared she would wander off. The waiting room had ancient grey and red lino pitted with cigarette burns and scuffed into holes. There were orange plastic chairs like at school, and these were filled with old men—really old drunk men with skin like textured wallpaper and stumpy brown teeth. There was one woman Mum's age reading *Cosmopolitan* and pretending not to notice the tramps as if she was really somewhere else. Stefanie noticed she had a huge bruise down the side of her face and she hugged her jaw every so often.

'I bet she never fell over—that one,' Stefanie whispered.

'The dental clinic?' the receptionist said again. 'There's a long wait, I'm afraid, it is Sunday morning. Can I have your details?' She moved her fingers across the grimy keyboard, cleaner round the e's and a's, blacker on x and z.

'No, no, we want casualty.' Amina kicked her. 'I mean the wards—intensive care—like that.'

The receptionist stopped tapping and looked exasperated. 'Enquiries and information is up by the main entrance.'

'Yes, we know that, we wanted—' Stefanie felt another kick from Amina and followed her out of the dental clinic into a corridor.

'There's a map—look.' Stefanie looked back into the waiting room through the round window. 'See?'

Stefanie nodded and they went ahead through another set of double doors. As they walked the floors got newer and cleaner, from polished lino to industrial carpet, and Stef reckoned they must be near the front. They got stopped by a security man in a brown nylon uniform but they smiled nicely at him and headed for the lift.

Chicksand Ward, Amina said, that was where Shahid was. At home her dad had written it on a bit of paper stuck up near the phone, and a phone number. Up here in the main part of the hospital it was full of people with flowers, visitors, mostly happy, but Stefanie saw a young man sitting in a plastic chair under a fire exit sign shaking with crying. He looked up and his eyes were so red.

'We should have bought flowers,' Stef said.

Amina didn't answer. She was walking fast down the corridor. A walk that was almost a run. Looking into the wards through their round windows as she passed.

'There!' Amina had found it. Chicksand Recovery Suite, it said. White on blue.

'Slow down.' Stefanie caught up with Amina. 'Just wait, get your breath back and calm down.' Amina was flushed with running.

'What if they've moved him? What if they won't let me in? What if Dad kills me?'

What if he's dead? Stef thought.

'What if he's dead?' Amina said. Suddenly the blood seemed to move away from under her skin, she was grey. Her eyes had shrunk.

'Amina?'

'I don't think I can do it, Stefanie. I think I'd better go home.'

'But we're here—right here. Look, Amina. I'm sure he's not dead.'

I'm lying, Stef thought. 'We'd know. You'd know, you'd be able to tell.'

'How?' Amina whispered. 'He could be dead and Dad gone home and then what?'

'It'll be OK. I'm sure.'

Amina breathed in deeply. 'I want to see him, even if he is dead. Right?'

'Right.'

Amina pushed on the door and it swung open.

Stef noticed the bleeping. The tiny squeaking of how many—four—heart monitors, one for each bed. Each bleep out of sync with the other. Each bed with one wired up human shell of a person. Each body with some bit of life making their bleeper bleep so you could tell they weren't dead. Maybe she should get one for her mum. It could bleep in time with the Motown.

Stef stayed by the door. She could see Shahid, his dad sitting by him staring into his face. Staring past the plastic tubes that snaked out of his nose, past the red cabbage face and the plastic stopper in his mouth.

Amina froze. 'He's dead.'

'He's bleeping. It's OK, Amina.' Stefanie hovered by the door, 'Go on.'

A nurse pushed through the door behind Stefanie. 'Are you family?' She sounded too tired to be angry. Amina stepped forward, Stefanie stepped back. The nurse smiled at Amina.

'He's just here,' and led her to the bedside.

Stefanie watched as Amina sat down opposite her father, frozen, grey. Then Amina started shaking. Started crying—Stef could tell—there were massive great tears just rolling, tumbling down her face. But she made no noise. There was no noise. Just the bleeping. Stefanie mouthed goodbye at Amina and waved but she didn't take her eyes off Shahid.

'You better go.' The nurse was holding the door open.

13

Stefanie stepped through the glass doors at the front of the hospital on to the pavement of the Whitechapel Road. The crowd from the march were still there, shouting at the police to get whoever had done it. 'You never do nothing for us.' One man—no, boy—had his face stuck right up against a policeman's face. The policeman was smiling. That nervous smiling.

'You don't care! You're bloody pigs!' The boy spat, coughing first, so it came up phlegmy like a naked shellfish. The policeman stopped smiling. Stefanie ran.

That boy should have spat at her, Stefanie thought. She knew. She knew exactly who'd done it. Stefanie stopped and looked back at the hospital and the crowd. She pictured them coming after her. She would have to tell someone. Mum would have to wait.

Stefanie walked and thought. Mostly about Becky. What if she knew—had known—all week? The clock on the old brewery building said eleven. With any luck

Becky's parents would be over their allotment. She started walking faster in case she changed her mind.

Becky's estate was busy. Someone had put a paddling pool out on the square of grass in the middle of the houses. Toddlers with no clothes and grass stuck to their bottoms squealed and splashed. There was a radio on but it was modern stuff. Stefanie almost missed the Motown. She smiled. It all looked so peaceful. Stefanie closed her eyes and she could see Martin spraying her and Becky with the hose. Not beating someone up. They'd all be laughing and soaking. But not hurt. Not bloody. Stefanie looked up at Becky's house. She hoped he wasn't in. She wished she had phoned first. Martin's window had a West Ham sticker and the curtains were drawn. Still in bed, she thought.

Stefanie walked up to the door. Her hand moved up to the bell and she remembered the loud slow chimes it made. She'd knock. But under the slightest pressure from her hand the door opened. Stefanie stood silent in the doorway. She could hear the plock plock plock of plastic sandals on lino from the kitchen.

'Becky?' she whispered. 'Becky.'

Becky turned into the hall wearing sunglasses, shorts, and a bikini top and carrying a plant sprayer.

'My God! Stef! Scared the life out of me!'

'It was open.'

'Yeah, I'm supposed to be doing the hanging baskets.' Becky squeezed the trigger of her plant sprayer. 'See? And you don't have to whisper. Mum and Dad are out.'

'Is Martin asleep?' Stefanie still whispered.

'Dunno. Shouldn't be, though. Martin!' Becky shouted up the stairs.

Stefanie froze.

'You OK? You look like you've been up all night. I wish I had. Boring as hell being grounded. And they've been stood over me going on and on about exams. What's been happening?'

Stefanie shrugged. She didn't know if Becky would believe her.

'Are you sure you're OK?' Becky took off her sunglasses and looked straight at Stef.

'Can we go over the park or something, Beck? I need to talk to you.'

Becky's mouth stretched wide into a grin. She gasped. Mock horror. 'You're never pregnant? Oh, Stef! You're not!'

Stefanie shook her head. She thought she was going to cry. Becky had no idea. It would be so much easier to keep things this way. Stefanie remembered Shahid bleeping. She remembered how he looked and how Amina had wept. Maybe she was just spreading the unhappiness around.

'I'm not pregnant, Beck.'

'Shame. It would've been fun, choosing the clothes. Getting a buggy.' Becky put her sunglasses back on. 'Only joking.'

Stef didn't smile.

'God! Stef! This touchy-touchy business. Did you get it off of Martin?'

'What do you mean?' Stefanie backed out of the hall and into the tiny front garden. Her eyes flicked up to Martin's window.

'I dunno. He's been edgy.' She followed Stefanie out and started squirting half heartedly at the hanging baskets. 'Jumpy. Like you.'

Becky gave Stef a squirt.

'I'm not jumpy.'

'Oh yeah?'

Stefanie looked at her reflection in Becky's sunglasses. Her hair was greasy and unbrushed and her eyes looked as scared as that zebra she'd seen on a nature programme. The one that had been ripped to pieces by a crocodile as it tried to cross a river.

'Can we go?'

'Give us a minute, Stef.' Becky went back inside. 'I just want to get a top.'

Stefanie went in after her and waited in the hall. She heard Becky moving around upstairs. A couple of doors banging and the flush of the toilet.

On the tiny table in the hall was a photo. Stefanie picked it up. It was Becky, Martin, and their mum and dad. They were on holiday, on a beach somewhere having a picnic. Becky waving, Mum unwrapping sandwiches. Dad holding a bottle of Coke, Martin squinting in the sun. They looked perfect. Like one of those families off the adverts. Glossy and colour and in focus.

Stefanie thought of the photo she'd seen at Amina's. That family already lopsided without a mother. Stefanie tried to project herself into a future when everything just went along and she kept her mouth shut. Becky would still be her friend and very soon Becky's parents would invite her round for tea again. For Sunday dinner sometimes and drives to Epping Forest. Stefanie swallowed. She sat down on the bottom stair still holding the photo.

She heard Becky's footsteps come thumping down the stairs behind her and she put the photo down. But it wasn't Becky. Martin was standing there, bare chested, tall.

'Hi, Stef.'

'Martin.' Stefanie hoped she wasn't giving anything away. She was sure he was looking into her, reading what she knew out of her insides. His chest was smooth. She was only as tall as his collar bone. Stefanie could see it almost straining at his brown skin. It looked like she could snap it if she wanted. She thought of her own bones. Stefanie felt fragile.

'Are you OK?' He scratched his head.

'I'm waiting for Beck.' Stefanie backed away.

'Mum and Dad won't be too pleased if they catch you round here. Leading our Becky astray.'

Normally Stef could take his wind-ups. But this morning she felt angry. 'I've done nothing wrong. I haven't!'

Martin's face seemed to slip. Just for a second. But Stefanie had seen it and he knew she'd seen it.

'I think I better go.' The blood was pumping round her head. 'Tell Beck . . . ' Stefanie turned for the door.

'Tell me what?' Becky came bounding down the stairs. 'What's up, Stef? Martin, are you winding her up?' Stefanie could tell from her face she had no idea. 'Martin, you leave her alone!'

'Beck, you stay out of this. What did Mum say? She said she wasn't having that little slut in our house again.'

'Martin!' Becky was angry.

'I'm going. All right? Becky, I'll see you. All right?' Stefanie thought she was going to cry.

'Stefanie!' Becky tried to follow her but Martin had closed the door. The hanging baskets shook as the door slammed. The kids in the paddling pool stared at Stefanie as she ran past.

Stefanie ran into the park and sat on the swings. Her trainers squeaked on the rubber matting and she breathed with the slow rhythm of the swing so she didn't cry. On the far side of the playground two little girls were lying on the roundabout face up looking at the sky. Stef didn't notice Becky until she came and sat down on the next swing.

'That was us,' Becky said. She was watching them too.

'Wasn't it!' Stef smiled at her.

113

They both swung for a bit.

'Sorry about Martin. He's a real bonehead sometimes.'

'Don't I know it.'

They swung a bit more. Stefanie opened her mouth to speak but couldn't. The longer she stayed quiet the longer everything would stay the same. Stay happy. But that was pretending. Just like Mum. Then her whole life, her whole friendship, would be built on lies. She'd be just like her mum. Stefanie gripped the chains of the swing until they dug hard into her hands and spoke.

'I know who did it, Beck. I know. It was Martin.'

Stefanie said it quickly so she wouldn't have to say it again. She thought Becky would jump up. Run off. Start shouting. But she said nothing. Becky was hardly swinging now. She sat letting the movement of the swing drag her legs and feet forward and back. Stefanie couldn't see her eyes, but she knew Becky believed her. Maybe she had known all along.

The playground began to fill up. The baby swings were full. Mothers and fathers lifting squealing babies in and out of the seats. Older children climbing on the spider's web. Jumping on it until it shook.

'Becky, I know it was him.' Stefanie said it again.

Becky stood up slowly. Stefanie looked up at herself in Becky's sunglasses.

'I have to tell, Beck. I wanted you to know first. But I have to tell someone.'

Becky shrugged. 'You just told me.' She sounded cold.

'No.' Stefanie shook her head. 'No, I have to tell *someone*. You know what I mean.'

'He's my brother, Stef. Even if he did do it . . . '

'You know it's true.' Stefanie shut her eyes. She sat up and lowered her voice. 'He nearly killed him!'

Becky pushed her sunglasses up her nose then folded her arms.

'You should have seen him, Beck! The boy in hospital! His family, Beck!'

'Yeah, well, what about our family then?' Becky's mouth tightened. She lowered her voice too. 'Mum and Dad. He was the one who was going to college . . . all that stuff . . . ' For a moment Stef thought she heard a catch in Becky's throat.

'Look, Stef.' Becky sat down next to her again. 'Why don't you just pretend nothing's happened? It'll all be over in a few weeks, that boy'll be walking around and no one needs to know. It'll be fine.'

Stefanie thought she'd cry. Becky didn't understand at all.

'Becky, he's dying. He's dying and I don't want to pretend anything. This isn't my fault, you know. Not mine!'

'But he's my brother!' Becky said. 'My brother.'

'I'll see,' Stefanie said. Very quietly.

Becky stood up and waited. Stefanie knew what she was waiting for. It was choosing time. Walk with Becky back to hers. Back to normal. Or stay here. On her own.

Becky turned and started walking. Slowly, deliberately. Plenty of time to catch up. Stefanie sat on the swing and watched her. After Becky had disappeared she uncurled her hands from the swing chains. Her palms were red and lumpy where the metal had cut into them. She sat quiet and rubbed them together until a woman with a toddler asked her if she was all right.

Stefanie went home.

14

Stefanie walked home the long way. She went to the marina and sat by the water for ages. She thought how much easier it would be to forget. To look away from Amina and walk along at school arm in arm with Becky laughing at last night's soaps. Keep your mouth shut. She had been friends with Becky from Year Seven.

She turned into the flats as the light was going. The first few dried up leaves were crispy on the paving and the shadows were long in the car park. The dust from the building site blew into her eyes and made them prickle. Hosna and her sisters were playing Barbies at the foot of the stairs, Mrs Menzies sat in a deck chair in front of her flat, surrounded by a horde of just-fed cats. Stefanie swung her bag so it bumped on the wall; it could have been any Sunday that had ever happened.

Stefanie took out the cardboard camera and took a picture of the little girls. The sun made their skin shine and their Barbies were all silver and pink. One of them held up her doll, 'Summer Wedding Princess Barbie, she is,' and twirled it. Stefanie thought of Amina marrying a spaceman and took another photo. She imagined the light and the metallic colours all moving, sparkling. Like on the insides of her eyes when she squeezed them hard shut.

Just the one picture left now.

Mrs Menzies folded shut her *News of the World* and stared at her. Stefanie stared right back, she hadn't done anything.

'Your mother . . . ' Stefanie didn't want to hear, Stefanie almost turned and walked out of the flats, out off somewhere else, somewhere where no one knew who she was, or what her mother was like. 'Your mother showed me your photographs.'

'What?' Stefanie couldn't have heard that right, she stopped a few metres in front of the old woman. 'What?'

'I think you mean pardon. "Pardon, missus," that's what you say!'

'Sorry, pardon, sorry. Mum, my mum, did that?'

'Not bad, I thought. Black and white though, bit dreary if you ask me, I prefer colour, myself. Nice woman, your mother, apart from that business with the music.'

Stefanie said nothing.

'Anyway you can do me now, if you like. I know you're a good girl for your mother. You should have asked nicely, girl. Manners, you know.'

Stefanie said nothing. Maybe she had that old people's disease that makes you mad. Stefanie watched the old woman grinning in the deck chair stroking a cat on her lap.

'Go on then, love.'

'My mum showed you my photos?'

'Well, that's what I said, dear, isn't it? Weeping, that poor woman was over you.'

Stefanie took the woman's picture quickly and ran up the stairs, three at a time. She thought her heart was going to burst. What had happened? Maybe Mum had seen the light, maybe she'd walk in and there'd be Mum all stood there in proper Mum clothes, navy blue, no heels, hoovering maybe. Mum would hear her come in and hug her. Tell her it would be OK. Becky had phoned. It was all right. It was all a mistake, Shahid was OK and Martin had spent all weekend on a football camp in Norfolk.

No, couldn't be, couldn't be. As she turned onto her landing she heard the music and slowed. Menzies was right, it wasn't as loud as normal but Stef could still hear it from here. 'If you're ready, come go with me.' It was the Staples Singers.

Stefanie turned the key and it felt like coming home from school. The music was on, the lights were on, Mum was home. No one had even checked if she'd slept in her bed. She put down her bag and sat at the kitchen table. The window was wide open, from when Stefanie had opened it yesterday morning. Nothing really changes, she thought, people don't change, I'm not changing, time just goes.

But the washing up had been done. She walked right over and stood by the sink, someone had done the washing up. The yellow gloves she had bought Mum last Mother's Day were lying, empty and used, on the drainer.

'Mum!' Stefanie dropped her bag and crashed through the flat. Mum was in the front room, not hoovering, as Stefanie had dreamed, but not swaying either. She was reading a magazine or something, smoking. 'Thin Thighs in Thirty Days!' it said. Mum looked up and walked across and turned the music down.

'Mum?' Stefanie pushed the hair up out of her face. Mum was looking at her, eye contact. 'Mum?'

'Call me Carole, love.' And she stubbed the cigarette out hard in the ashtray so it concertinaed into itself. 'I'm sorry about all that, with the photos . . . all that . . . me . . . '

'What is this, Mum?' Stefanie sat down, she didn't think she could get used to Carole.

'I knew you'd gone, I'm just very glad you're back.' And she smiled, not just the regular pretend smile.

'Mum, did you really show my pictures to Mrs Menzies?'

'I showed them to the nice reporter too, that one with the shiny bob. You know—dark auburn she is—out of a box, I reckon. Anyway, she thinks you're not bad at all. She reckons you're pretty good.'

Stefanie wanted to smile. She really wanted to. But instead she burst into tears, loud non-stop sobbing. Just like Mum. Mum got up and hugged her, turned the music up and hugged her and Stefanie cried.

When the music stopped Stefanie talked. Stefanie talked and Mum listened. She really did listen as well, not the fake smiling and nodding which was the best Stefanie could usually hope for. Stefanie had to pinch herself.

'I don't want anything to change, Mum, but I can't do it. I can't just walk around knowing.'

'Sleep on it,' Mum said. 'Look at you! You can hardly keep your eyes open.'

'But, Mum, Becky's going to hate me.'

Mum stroked her hair. 'Tell you what. In the morning, first thing, you tell me what you want to do. We can go to the police, to whoever—do nothing if you want. Your choice.' Mum lit up another cigarette. 'I can't make it all better. If you don't know that by now . . . ' She trailed off.

'If he died I'd hate myself.'

'You've got me, love. Remember that. I'm not entirely useless.'

They both smiled.

'I don't want to be useless, Stef. I want to be like those mums off of the telly. Cooking stuff and coping.'

'Just be . . . ' Stefanie stopped. She was going to say be yourself, but what she wanted was someone more responsible, less self obsessed. 'Just be like you are now, like this. Please?'

'I'll try, I will. We'll manage, Stef.'

Stefanie lay in her own bed with the smell of the sheets and the dark shapes of the things in her room. She tried to make her head empty, no Shahid, no Martin, no Becky.

Stefanie turned around under the duvet, letting the tired and the sleep just fall over her, making patterns come in the darkness by just staring. Brown and dark red and deep grey patterns—moving, some of them. Stefanie had made her choice, that wasn't so hard. It was tomorrow at school that would be hard and all the days after that. It was life that was hard.

For a few seconds before she drifted into sleep Stefanie knew what her mum was scared of. Stefanie thought of her photos and promised herself that whatever was going to happen now, she wouldn't be.